Mirror of Danger

Mirror of Danger

by Pamela Sykes

THOMAS NELSON INC., PUBLISHERS

Nashville, Tennessee / New York, New York

Copyright © 1973, 1974 by Pamela Sykes

All rights reserved under International and Pan-American Conventions. Published by Thomas Nelson Inc., Nashville, Tennessee. Manufactured in the United States of America.

Second printing

For Veryan

Library of Congress Cataloging in Publication Data

Sykes, Pamela.
   Mirror of danger.

   SUMMARY: An orphan, come to live with distant cousins, suddenly finds herself getting glimpses into the past as she meets a mysterious girl, Alice.
   Published in 1973 under title: Come back, Lucy.
   [1. Space and time—Fiction. 2. Orphans—Fiction] I. Title.
PZ7.S9833Mi3   [Fic]   73–17102
ISBN 0–8407–6373–5

Chapter One

"AND I know you're going to be very brave—er—
Lucy, and sensible," said Mr. Peel the lawyer.

Lucy fidgeted impatiently. They'd been saying
things like that for the last week. As far as they knew
she *had* been brave. And as for being sensible, what
was she supposed to be sensible about? She decided
that now was the time to ask.

"Sensible about what?"

"Everything, dear," said fat comfortable Mrs. Belling from next door. "When somebody passes on,
there are always changes. Unsettling at first, but
people soon accept them."

Lucy knew that by 'people' Mrs. Belling meant
Lucy herself. Then why couldn't she say so? And
why did she say 'passed on' when everybody knew
she meant 'died'? Aunt Olive had died. She was
dead. *Dead.* That was the whole awful trouble. But
it didn't help when everybody used the words they
didn't mean, and kept looking at each other over her
head, and having quiet hurried conversations which
ended just as Lucy appeared.

"What sort of changes?" she asked suspiciously,
her voice coming out much louder than she had intended because she was so anxious to know.

Mr. Peel tut-tutted gently, and Mrs. Belling put a strong plump arm around Lucy. "There now, there's no need to get into a state. We're all here to help you, you know. Mr. Thomas, I wonder if perhaps you'd explain——?"

Mr. Thomas was the vicar. Lucy had attended his services every week for as long as she could remember. He was a calm direct person. She looked at him hopefully but saw that even he was a little uncomfortable. "Your aunt," he said, "though she had no idea this state of affairs was to come about so soon or so suddenly, had made provision for you." Dear kind Aunt Olive. She would have. "Apart from a few bequests"—here Mrs. Belling sniffed—"everything which was hers now becomes yours."

"Everything?" echoed Lucy, hope suddenly springing like a tiny new blade of grass forcing its way through concrete. "You mean, the house?"

"The house, and everything in it."

Lucy gave a little sigh. For the first time since the dreadful moment when she'd heard the news she stopped feeling as if she were walking about in a black fog with no top or bottom or sides to it. Home, The Shrubbery, was safe. Not only home, but the dear familiar things in it.

"Technically, that is," said Mr. Peel. "Unfortunately your aunt was no business woman and I'm afraid her affairs were in a sad muddle. There was very little money, and——"

"But it's not the money that matters!" cried Lucy.

"Unfortunately it matters very much," Mr. Peel said dryly. "Miss Boyd was not at all well off when she died. I did try to explain the matters to her several times," he added in an excusing voice to Mr. Thomas over Lucy's head, "but she had little grasp of figures, and the situation at the moment is far from satisfactory." He looked again at Lucy. "Our main concern is to see that there is enough for you until you can earn a living for yourself."

"Oh I'm sure there will be," Lucy said confidently. "I'll be very careful. I'll manage." Aunt Olive had often said, "You're going to make a good little manager one day." Now the day, it seemed, was here.

Mr. Peel looked astonished. "My dear young lady, at eleven years old it's not for you to worry your head about such things."

"Not me? Then who?"

"I, for one," Mr. Thomas broke in in his quiet voice, "because I'm one of your trustees. These are grown-up people appointed to look after the money of younger people until they're old enough to look after it for themselves. The Trustees of your money, appointed by your Aunt Olive, are Mr. Peel, the Bank, and myself. Between us we shall look after everything and you won't have to worry about it."

"What about paying bills and things?"

"We shall do all that."

"But——" Lucy began.

Mrs. Belling's arm tightened round her. "Stop fretting, duckie. Plenty of time for bills when you're a bit older. You'll see enough of them then. Let the gentlemen look after everything. Then you won't need to worry, wherever you are."

"What do you mean wherever I am? I shall be here, at home," said Lucy firmly. "Just like I always have been."

"What, a little girl live all by herself?" said Mrs. Belling.

"But you'd be on one side of me, and Mrs. Thomas on the other. I wouldn't really be alone."

"It's quite out of the question, Lucy," said Mr. Thomas. "You must see that."

"Even if it were possible in the practical sense," Mr. Peel added, "I'm afraid the first thing we must do is to sell the house."

"Sell the house?"

"I'm afraid so. Otherwise there won't be any money."

As matters were explained to her, Lucy's little springing hope withered and died. The dark fog returned. It all made such terrible sense. Everybody must have some money in the bank. Aunt Olive had had hardly any, and Lucy had none of her own. In order to get some, something would have to be sold. The only thing that could be sold was the house and the things in it. So the house and furniture would go up for auction as soon as possible. Some stranger would simply bid more money than another and the house would be his.

"But what will happen to me?" Lucy asked at last in a very small voice.

"There now," said Mr. Thomas. "Did you know you had some cousins?"

"No," said Lucy, not caring.

"Well, you have. Distant ones, but definitely related. We've got in touch with them, and they've very kindly asked you to spend the Christmas holidays with them."

The thought of Christmas anywhere else but at home and with anyone else but Aunt Olive was almost too dreadful to be borne, but while she could still use her voice Lucy had to know the answers to some more questions. "What about after Christmas?"

"Well after Christmas—we'll see. Perhaps you'd like to go on staying with them if you're happy there. Otherwise I'm sure we can make other arrangements."

The phrase 'other arrangements' brought on more and darker fog. Lucy twisted herself round to face Mrs. Belling. "Couldn't I come and live with you? For always." She'd been staying in her house since Aunt Olive had gone to hospital suddenly in the night.

"Afraid not, duckie. We haven't the space, have we, when you think? Young Bill's sleeping on the settee now to make room for you, and there'll be another of us any day now. I don't really see how we could manage it."

"I suppose not," Lucy said miserably. Mrs. Belling had a loud voice, and always smelt faintly of tomato soup, but she was kind. And most important of all, familiar.

The talk about Lucy's future went on and on. They told her how nice her cousins sounded: an artistic mother, a father who was an architect, and three children round about her own age. The parents had written kind and welcoming letters to the trustees. Now that things looked settled, Mrs. Long, the aunt, would be writing to Lucy herself. Soon they would come in a car to fetch her away.

'Who shall we send to fetch her away, fetch her away, fetch her away?' The jingle echoed crazily round Lucy's foggy head. There was so much to think about that she couldn't think at all. There were so many questions that she didn't know which one to ask first. Everything had been so unexpected that she felt a little sick.

Mrs. Belling gave her one last squeeze and said, "*I* know someone who'd like a nice cup of tea." Mrs. Belling thought cups of tea were the best cure for everything. She bustled into the kitchen, leaving Lucy behind. A tear oozed out of her left eye.

9

"Now, now," said Mr. Peel, seeing it. "You said you were going to be brave and sensible."

"No, you said that," Lucy answered. Now she knew why.

*　　*　　*

She would have been even more fearful of the future had she heard a conversation between Mrs. Belling and Mr. Thomas a day or two later.

Mrs. Belling was energetically polishing the faded paintwork in the dining-room of The Shrubbery ("Miss Boyd's house was always spotless. No one shall see it otherwise"). Mr. Thomas called in for a word.

"How's Lucy?"

Mrs. Belling stopped her work. "Very peaky still. Right off her food. I'm worried about her, Vicar."

"Has she cried yet?"

"Not a tear. So much better if she could. Get it out of her system."

"How does she feel about the visit to her relations?"

"Not looking forward to it, poor mite. No reason why she should, is there? Christmas with strangers. It doesn't seem right, somehow."

"It's Christmas with a young family. You must think of it that way, Mrs. Belling."

Mrs. Belling scooped a smear of polish on to her duster. "A family, Vicar, is just what Lucy is not used to." She rubbed fiercely at the window-sill. "You know that as well as I do."

"Of course, Mrs. Belling, of course." Mr. Thomas began to walk up and down the room. "But it's what she should have been used to, and this is a splendid chance to put things right." Mrs. Belling rubbed on, without speaking. "After all, I don't know what we should have done without the kind offer of these people. They're under no moral obligation to take an interest in Lucy. Yet they've said that if she settles in happily with their children, they'll consider bringing her up as one of their own."

"You can't say fairer than that," Mrs. Belling admitted. "All the same, I don't see it working out. Do you truly, Vicar?" Mrs. Belling abandoned the window-sill to face him squarely. "Miss Boyd was a dear lady, and she did her best by the child. But she was elderly, and elderly in her ways. Lucy wasn't brought up like other children, and she doesn't act like them, so it's no good pretending she does." After which pronouncement, rather red in the face she went back to her polishing.

"I quite understand," said Mr. Thomas gently. "Believe me, Mrs. Belling. But what else were we to do? Where else could she go?"

Mrs. Belling had no answer to this. Instead she asked, still rubbing vigorously, "And suppose things don't work out with these relations? What then?"

"I very much hope they will. But if not . . . we shall have to see. We might manage a boarding-school——"

"A *boarding-school!*" Mrs. Belling was very shocked. "*Lucy at a boarding-school?*"

"It's a solution," said Mr. Thomas, almost apologetically. "There are some very good ones, I believe, which will keep the children during the holidays——"

But Mrs. Belling would hear no more. "The very idea! Little Lucy sent right away to a place like that!" Then she remembered who she was talking to. She went redder than ever. "I'm sorry, Vicar. I shouldn't have spoken out like that. And it's not for me to say, anyhow. It's none of my concern."

11

"Lucy is the concern of *all* of us," said Mr. Thomas firmly. He patted Mrs. Belling on the shoulder because she was gustily blowing her nose. "We only want to do what's best for her."

*   *   *

It was hard for Lucy to remember this through the next days. They swirled with the black fog. When she felt brave enough she asked questions.

"How do I know the cousins want me?" she said to Mrs. Belling.

"Now would they have asked you to go there if they didn't?"

Lucy was not satisfied with this sensible answer. The unknown uncle and aunt probably only felt it their duty to ask her to stay. They probably didn't want her at all. Nor would their children.

"If they want me to go there, why haven't they asked me before?"

"They didn't know about you, duckie. That's why. Now sit down like a good girl and have some tea."

Lucy sat down like a good girl but the tea did not interest her. She sighed heavily.

"There now," said Mrs. Belling. "Drink up and you'll feel better. Your aunt wouldn't have wanted you to fret. She was always one for looking on the bright side."

"There isn't a bright side to look on," said Lucy.

"Nonsense!" Mrs. Belling sounded brisk. "You'll be meeting new people. Later you'll be going to school and——"

"School?" said Lucy, in horror. "School?"

"But of course. Everybody goes to school. It's the law."

12

Of course she was right. But in her misery and despair, Lucy had not thought of this. She had never been to school in her life and never wanted to. Aunt Olive had been a teacher in rather a grand private girls' school till she had given up a career to look after Lucy after her parents had been killed in an accident. As there had not been enough money to send her to the same kind of school, and Aunt Olive disapproved of state schools, she had educated Lucy at home herself, except for a weekly dancing class with dear old Miss Thwaites.

"*School!*" said Lucy again. Even the thought of it made her shudder. She'd never be able to face all those strange children. She had seen them waiting in giggling groups for the bus. Often she suspected the giggling was about her, and Aunt Olive. She was not sure why this should be so, but she knew Aunt Olive had felt the same because she used to hustle her along murmuring, "Pay no attention. They don't know any better."

"You'll be able to play games," said Mrs. Belling encouragingly.

Lucy suppressed a shudder. She'd seen the boys playing football in their filthy muddy striped jerseys, and the girls thundering up and down the hockey field, or cheering each other on at netball. Not what she and Aunt Olive had meant by games at all.

When Mr. Peel next called he explained that though most of the furniture would have to be sold, Lucy could choose one or two favourite pieces to keep till she was old enough to need them. She could also take away with her some smaller things that she would particularly like to have with her now. "Not too many, mind," Mr. Peel warned, seeing her face suddenly light.

"How many?"

"I think all your belongings should fit into one trunk," said Mr. Peel.

Lucy spent a whole day choosing. The furniture was easy. Aunt Olive's desk, a small table that had stood by the fire and had a chess board built into the top of it; a little round footstool, the miniature chest of drawers made with patterned wood, Lucy's own bed.

It was more difficult to decide what to take with her. She wanted all the things that were especially Aunt Olive's and which they had shared. Without hesitation she took an old family photograph album they'd often looked at together, the spillikins, the playing-cards, both the plain and Happy Families, the chess set.

Then she turned to the bookshelf. Alice in Wonderland, of course. The E. Nesbits, A Child's Garden of Verses, Babar the Elephant, The Jungle Book, the Beatrix Potters . . . the trunk became more and more full. It was hard to leave any of the old favourites behind. Her last search was through the 'treasure drawer'. Here were kept Aunt Olive's own old paint-box of polished wood with its tiny pans of paint—almost empty now—the slender brushes, the sliding compartment for a sketching-block. The mother-of-pearl fish counters must come, the dance-programmes with minute tasselled pencils attached that had belonged to Aunt Olive's mother, the soft leather writing case with gold initials on it.

Everything Aunt Olive had owned had been like herself, fragile, delicate and beautifully made. "You won't find things in the shops like this these days," she had often said of her possessions and Lucy knew this to be true.

She was wondering what else she could possibly fit

in when a sudden noise downstairs set her heart knocking. She had thought she was quite alone in the house. Footsteps. Then Mr. Thomas's head round the door. "I'm so sorry Lucy. I must have startled you. What are you doing here all by yourself?"

She explained. He listened with a grave face. "I'd like to take everything," she finished wistfully.

"But you won't need everything," said Mr. Thomas, his eye running over the things piled into the trunk. "You'll be much too busy doing things with your cousins."

"No I won't," said Lucy quickly.

"Which you'll enjoy once you've got to know them," went on Mr. Thomas as if she hadn't spoken.

"I don't want to know them," Lucy muttered.

"Now that's a stupid thing to say." Mr. Thomas lowered himself into an armchair. "It sounds almost as if you've made up your mind not to like them before you've even met."

As this was exactly what Lucy had decided she said nothing, but fiddled with a hand-painted Chinese fan.

"You know," Mr. Thomas began again, and Lucy could tell from his voice that he was thinking very carefully before each word, "you've had a wonderful life with Aunt Olive, but things couldn't have gone on for ever as they were."

"You mean she'd have died anyway?"

"No," said Mr. Thomas. "I mean that you're a big girl now. It's high time you went out into the world to find out what life's about."

"I don't want to," said Lucy.

"I know," said Mr. Thomas gravely, "that's half the trouble. Your aunt was a dear person but she wasn't young and she tended to look backwards."

"So did I," said Lucy. "I like looking backwards."

15

Mr. Thomas nodded. "Just what I mean. It's time you looked forward."

"Like how?" Lucy asked sullenly, fiddling with the fan.

"Like being prepared to be friends with your cousins."

"How can I when I don't know anything about them?"

"I can help you there," said Mr. Thomas as if he hadn't noticed that Lucy was being sulky, "as it happens I had a long talk with your aunt on the telephone last night, so I can tell you quite a lot. . ."

Although Lucy tried not to listen, she couldn't help hearing about her aunt who used to design costumes for the stage, but had already thrown herself into local affairs. About Patrick the eldest child, Rachel about her own age and Bill, only nine. Recently the family had moved to a big house on the outskirts of London. All sorts of plans were being made for Christmas. . . .

At this point Lucy managed to let Mr. Thomas's voice float away. Since Aunt Olive's illness she had discovered this was a very useful thing to be able to do. The trick was to think yourself very hard into some other time and place so that what was actually happening at the moment became less important. It had helped enormously when the news was bad, then worse, then unbearable. It had saved her at the funeral. Instead of seeing red-eyed Mrs. Belling beside her, and the sad grey rain outside, and hearing Mr. Thomas's gentle comforting words, she had thought and thought herself back to an evening in the summer when she and Aunt Olive had played croquet. The kitten from over the road had stalked into the garden and joined in the game, patting the balls so seriously, that it had made them laugh and laugh. Late orange sunlight, filled with birdsong, lit the crimson antirrhinums and drew long shadows across the neat lawn. That had been a happy time. It had been almost surprising to Lucy to find herself in the churchyard, the funeral over, everyone looking at her anxiously, almost as if she were ill.

Though being ill with Aunt Olive could be fun, too, she now remembered. It was then that the old albums were brought out and together they had studied the faded brown photographs of young gentlemen escorting young ladies in long tight uncomfortable dresses, as they picnicked by the river, played croquet, or merely sat about stiffly in drawing-rooms so crowded with furniture that there seemed scarcely room for people. Aunt Olive knew the names of everyone in the pictures. Her stories about them were so entertaining that it was easy to forget you had a sore throat, or a headache. Lucy felt she knew the people in the photographs almost as well as they knew each other, and would be quite at home with them. . . .

"——and I've no doubt you'll make other friends of your own——." Mr. Thomas's voice came floating back. "I know it's difficult to believe now, but soon—sooner than you'd believe possible—this bad time will seem a long time ago. You may even come to see that in a strange way things have turned out for the best."

Lucy, jolted back to the present, gripped the fan so hard that she afterwards found she had broken it. "No!" she exclaimed with sudden violence, for whatever Mr. Thomas had been saying before, about this she was certain he was wrong.

He stood up. "We shall see. Now I'm going round to have a word with Mrs. Belling. Suppose you come with me."

17

She didn't want to go with him to Mrs. Belling's bright noisy kitchen where the children would be, but Mr. Thomas was cheerfully firm and she found herself leaving the house with him.

Very soon a van came to take those items Lucy had chosen to a store. The day after, men from an auctioneer's firm put numbers on everything else and a large red 'For Sale' notice in the garden. After they'd gone the house smelt of stale cigarettes instead of live flowers and pot-pourri. It looked and felt quite unlike itself with its bare windows (the curtains were tied into bundles on the hall floor) and the remaining furniture huddled unnaturally, as if it were nervous, against the walls. Lucy was glad to stay next door with Mrs. Belling.

There was the beginning of trouble about the trunk being so full that there was hardly any room for clothes. "And what we do get in will be crushed!" wailed Mrs. Belling. "Take a few things out, duckie, and make space for this nice new coat and muff your Aunt gave you just before—just before——"

In spite of Mrs. Belling's distress, Lucy remained very firm. "No," she said. And in answer to further protests: "I don't want to talk about it."

One morning a long letter for Lucy came from her newly-discovered Aunt Gwen. The writing was large and thick and dark, as if the words had been written in a great hurry. 'Our very dear Lucy,' it began. 'We're so looking forward to our meeting next week. . . .'

'Oh, were they?' thought Lucy. 'More than I am.' She skipped a page. '. . . so we'll leave it to you to make the first move. Now, you'll want to know something about us, I'm sure, so . . .'

Lucy refolded the thick pages, unread, and stuffed them into her newly-acquired writing case. She *didn't* want to know anything about them. Nothing at all. She'd find out next week all right. Till then, she'd forget they existed.

The goodbyes were dreadful. Saying it to the house was not as bad as she'd expected, but Mr. Thomas was another matter. Lucy, in her best red woollen dress, all ready to leave, hung on to his hand as if she could never let it go. He put on a surprised expression. "What's all this? Aren't you coming back to see us?"

"Will I be able to?"

"Why not?" said Mr. Thomas. "We shall all be here waiting to hear how you're getting on, and looking forward to a visit. And you'll want to see Mrs. Belling's new baby when it arrives, won't you? I'll write to you, soon. Meanwhile, you do your best to enjoy yourself. You know what I mean." He looked very hard at her. "I know you won't let us down, Lucy."

She came the nearest to crying, then, than she ever had. But she managed not to.

Mrs. Belling was the crying one. When the expected car slid to a stop outside the gate, tears ran down her cheeks. This was awful. It made Lucy panicky inside. She flung herself at Mrs. Belling. "Don't make me go! Don't let them take me!"

"Now, now, duckie, there's no need for you to take on, just because I'm a silly old woman." She unpicked Lucy's clutching hands.

Uncle Peter was tall and quiet and slow. Aunt Gwen was tall and gay and quick in everything she did. She exactly matched her handwriting. "Lucy!" she cried, her scarlet cloak swinging from her shoulders as she leapt from the car. "How lovely to see you! And what a pretty dress!"

Lucy shook hands gravely, "How do you do?" she said, as Aunt Olive had taught her.

"This must be Mrs. Belling!" Aunt Gwen went on gaily. "How d'you do, Mrs. Belling? We've heard all about you from Mr. Thomas—so kind, you've been—is this your luggage, Lucy?" And before she could answer; "Pete, there's a great trunk here, can you cope?—Oh, this must be Mr. Thomas——"

Lucy stared. The only aunt she had ever known had been Aunt Olive. It seemed almost impossible that this person could be the same kind of relation. There was a good deal of grown-up talking. The trunk was edged into the boot of the car by Mr. Thomas and Uncle Peter. Aunt Gwen talked louder and faster than anyone till suddenly she looked at her watch and exclaimed, "Heavens, is that the time? We ought to have left hours ago!"

Uncle Peter smiled indulgently, and packed her into the front of the car, Lucy into the back. There was hardly time for any more goodbyes. One minute all was voices and waving hands and confusion. The next, The Shrubbery was out of sight. Everything and everybody that Lucy had ever known were becoming farther away with every moment.

Uncle Peter drove with silent concentration, but Aunt Gwen hardly stopped talking in her cheerful, disconnected way. "Such an upheaval for you . . . must be dozens of questions you want to ask . . . let me tell you about the family."

"You did. You wrote," Lucy murmured.

Her aunt went gaily on as if she hadn't heard her. "I hope you like pop music because they're all mad about it, and Patrick's saving up for one of those make-it-yourself record playing kits. You know?" Lucy didn't know. She'd never heard of such a thing. "He and Bill fight all the time, unless they're gang-ing up on Rachel. She can't wait for you to come to make the numbers even. You'll find her rather a tomboy. I wish I could get her to wear pretty clothes like you but nothing in this world would get her out of jeans. . ."

As Aunt Gwen rattled on Lucy stared out of the window at the grey December landscape flashing by and deliberately didn't listen. Such a wave of longing for Aunt Olive swept over her that she could actually see, instead of houses and streets and trees, the drawing-room and The Shrubbery as it had been this time a year ago, reflected in the glass of the car-window. There was the walnut desk, the leaping fire, and Aunt Olive kneeling on the hearth-rug wrapping a cardigan for Mrs. Belling in Christmas paper.

The curtains were warmly drawn against the chill evening, and the little green tree, sparkling with many-coloured lights and delicate ornaments filled the curve of the window. The scene was so real that Lucy felt she was actually there, part of it. Instead of the thrumming of the engine and Aunt Gwen's enthusiastic voice she heard the creaking of the fire, the crackle of paper, and Aunt Olive quietly reminiscing about Christmas in the old days. Instead of the petrol-and-leather smell of the car, there was the exciting Christmasy mixture of wood smoke and pine needles, pot-pourri, the cold blue scent of early indoor hyacinths. . .

With a shock, Lucy realised the car had stopped. Uncle Peter was opening the door for her, Aunt Gwen was laughing. "Wake up, Lucy! You've been dreaming. We've arrived!"

Chapter Two

Lucy, climbing from the car, saw that they were in a square with large houses on all sides of it. Each house had an imposing gate and a short curved drive. In the middle of the square was a garden where a round pool reflected the crimson setting sun. She gazed round her. Although the square seemed grander than their road at home, there was something comfortably familiar about the solid gabled houses.

"A bit like The Shrubbery," she murmured to herself.

Uncle Peter heard her. "Quite right, Lucy, built about the same time. Fancy you noticing! None of my three would have. Did you hear that, Gwen? Lucy saw at once that———"

But Aunt Gwen had already snatched Lucy's hand case from the car. "Hurry up, Pete, we don't want to keep her chatting out here, it's cold. Come on, Lucy, we'll go and meet the others." She leapt two at a time up the steps to the front door, her cloak swinging. Lucy followed her slowly, her feet wanting more and more to turn and run in the other direction. Inside the house a blare of mixed sounds hit them. It seemed to be a mixture of shrill argument with a background of a bellowing bass voice and some loud booming music.

"Oh dear," said Aunt Gwen, "Home sweet Home!" but she laughed as she said it. Lucy stiffened. Aunt Olive had hated loud noises, so Lucy herself had come to dislike them as well. Anything less home-like than this was hard to imagine.

One voice became clear above all others. "If you don't stop that racket, young Billy, I'll clobber you one!"

The end of the sentence was drowned by a re-newed drumming. As if in answer to the attack two American male voices were raised in furious dispute: "Drop those guns!"... "I'll see you dead first!" "Boom! Boom! Boom!" "Patrick, I mean it!" Another exasperated voice,—"Can't you stop fight-ing, you two?"

"Children!" exclaimed Aunt Gwen. Nobody heard her. Lucy shrank against the wall. Beside her was an enormous red and yellow painting of nothing recognisable. Another—blue and green swirls—hung on the opposite wall. Beneath it was a table such as Lucy had never seen before: large, angular, of very pale wood. She could glimpse similar furniture through the other door of the sitting-room, from which the vivid colours of the curtains and cushions seemed to leap towards her. What a horrible, horrible place!

Uncle Peter joined them. His voice overcame all others. "Shut up, the lot of you!"

Abruptly the arguing ceased. The American ranted on accompanied by the drums. Then there were only the drums. Finally they, too, were cut off. Three figures erupted into the hall. They all wore their hair below their ears, blue jeans and large chunky sweaters in varying bright colours. Lucy stared at them.

"Sorry Mum, we didn't hear you arrive!" the green-jerseyed figure explained. You could tell she was a girl only by her voice. "Where's——?" She caught sight of Lucy. "Oh, there you are. You must be Lucy. I'm Rachel, these two savages are my brothers Patrick and Bill."

The tallest savage grinned and held out a hand. "She's a fine one to call anyone a savage! You wait, you'll find out. Come here, young Bill, and be introduced properly." Patrick gave his brother a shove forward.

"Hello, I'm Bill, why are you so dressed up?" asked the smallest boy in one breath.

"Because she's *not* a savage," said Aunt Gwen quickly. "Come on in Lucy, and don't take any notice of them. Patrick, give your father a hand with the trunk. Bill, do stop staring. Rachel, my angel, did you remember to put the potatoes on?"

"Help! I forgot. Not the *on* bit——"

"——but the off. I thought I could smell something," said Aunt Gwen. "Another black pan! Never mind, I'll see about it. Take Lucy upstairs and show her everything." She peeled off her cloak as she spoke, flung it on to a chair in the hall and whisked through a door. Lucy glimpsed a large kitchen, cluttered and steamy.

"This way," said Rachel from the foot of the stairs. There was nothing to do but plod up behind her. Rachel threw open a door. "This is us."

"*Us?*" Lucy stopped on the threshold unable to believe the implications of the phrase, but Rachel was already inside the room. "This is my bed, and that's yours over there. I've emptied the two top drawers of the dressing table, and you can have

24

whichever side of the wardrobe you like. You can hardly share a desk, can you? So I haven't moved anything out of mine. Perhaps later, when—if—" Rachel hesitated. "Don't you think it's a nice room?" she finished proudly, watching Lucy's face.

It was a fairly nice room. Or would have been if only one person were to occupy it. But two? Was Lucy really expected to *share* a bedroom? The place where you kept your most private possessions, thought your private thoughts, dressed, undressed, everything. . . . She could hardly believe it.

"Do you mean," she asked, not moving, "that we're going to be in here together?"

Some of the pride went out of Rachel's face. "That was the idea."

"I'm—I'm——" Lucy struggled for words, "er— used to sleeping alone, you see," she finished feebly.

Rachel nodded. "So am I, but Dad's busy doing things to the house as fast as he can so that we can use more of it. Till then—" her smile was polite if not warm—"we've got to share."

I won't, Lucy told herself, I won't, I won't, I won't! "Don't you have a spare room?"

"We have, but you should see it! I'll show you later. Would you like to unpack now?"

"No, thank you," said Lucy. She wasn't going to unpack in this room, just in case there might somehow be a chance of getting somewhere to sleep alone. She remembered the look of the house from outside. "What about any attics?" she enquired.

"Three," said Rachel. "But not habitable. At least that's what Dad says. We've been having terrific arguments. . . . I'll show you where the bathroom is."

Lucy locked herself in the bathroom. The sound of the bolt sliding in to its socket was the best thing she'd heard since she left The Shrubbery. For the first time she felt she could take a deep breath. One thing was certain: she wasn't going to live in this house for one minute longer than was absolutely necessary. It wasn't a home at all. Just the remains of a comfortable old house now filled with ugly furniture and ridiculous pictures and noisy people who didn't even know you had to be alone sometimes.

Supper was an uproarious affair. There were jokes about the absence of potatoes. Nobody seemed to be cross with Rachel for having wasted a whole panful. Aunt Gwen, who actually seemed to find the situation funny, said at last, "Stop getting at her. Anyone can make mistakes. What about the time the bathroom tap was left on?"

Everyone looked at Patrick, who grinned sheepishly but could only defend himself by saying, "Anyway the ceiling didn't come down like you said it would."

"No thanks to you," said his father.

"But you swore at the time——" began Patrick.

The loud and cheerful argument which followed was almost drowned by another between Rachel and Bill. It apparently concerned some tune that was, or was not, in the top ten. Rachel turned to Lucy suddenly and asked, "I'm right, aren't I?"

"I don't know," she had to admit. She and Aunt Olive had never listened to pop music.

Aunt Gwen said, "It's been quite a day for Lucy. I expect she's too tired to give her mind to anything much except early bed. Which," she added, "wouldn't hurt the rest of you either." Her words fell into one of the brief silences and caused instant uproar, but Uncle Peter was quietly firm. "Anyone downstairs after nine o'clock will do an hour's paper-scrubbing tomorrow," he added casually.

This brought groans of protest but seemed to end the matter. Even these noisy rebellious children sometimes did as they were told then. As the clock struck nine they trailed up to bed still grumbling and protesting but without malice.

"Anything rather than do a stint on those awful walls," Rachel explained to Lucy in their room.

"What walls?"

"Come with me, I'll show you. You asked me about the spare room." She flung open a door on the landing. "Now you know why no one can sleep in it yet."

The room was indeed in a terrible state. Furniture was piled in the middle of it and covered with dust sheets. Parts of the walls were bare down to the plaster, but others were tatty with hanging strips of paper showing layer after layer of different colours beneath. "Dad's dead keen about everything being done properly," Rachel went on, "so it's taking ages, and awful to do. It's his ultimate deterrent."

Lucy examined the top layer of wallpaper, a design of roses and looped blue ribbons. "What was wrong with it as it was?"

Rachel made a face at the design. "Well, look at it! Enough to give anyone nightmares."

"I like it," said Lucy.

"Do you?" Rachel seemed honestly surprised. "It wouldn't go well in a modern room though, would it?"

"But this is a Victorian house. Your father told me. So why must its rooms be modern?"

"Because that's Dad's *thing*: modernising old houses." It would be, thought Lucy. "He's very good at it. There was a big article in a glossy magazine about him not long ago with lots of before-and-after photos of places he'd done. He's got some good ideas for this room too. He's going to put books where the fireplace is now, and all this wall is to be a built-in cupboard except for a sort of counter that will do as a dressing table or a desk."

Lucy thought it sounded dreadful, but Rachel was looking at her expectantly so she tried to think of something truthful but not too tactless to say.

"Won't it seem rather bare?"

"Yes, lovely. Lots of room for *being* in. And of course much more practical for cleaning. You've got to think of things like that too, Dad says."

Really, the way she showed off about her father! And all because he spent his life trying to change the lovely old houses into ugly new-looking ones. She ought to be ashamed instead of proud. "I don't think it sounds very homey," Lucy said, as Rachel led the way from the room.

"Nor do I."

Just for a foolish moment Lucy was so sure someone had whispered those words from within the spare room that she turned back to make sure there was no one in it. But of course there wasn't. She knew that really. It must have been her own tired mind imagining what Aunt Olive would have said had she been with them.

Back in the bedroom she took her nightdress and wash things from her hand-case and made for the bathroom. The door was locked. Loud sounds of splashing and shouting came from within. Lucy trailed back to the bedroom.

"The boys have bagged the bathroom I suppose?" queried Rachel, who had discarded her jersey and jeans already. "Never mind, we'll give them five minutes and go and shout them out." She casually peeled off her vest. "It'll be nice to have another girl on my side. It's usually two against one." She started to take off her pants.

Lucy looked quickly away. She had never seen anyone undress completely before. And after all, she and Rachel were absolute strangers. Being relations didn't count if you'd only met that evening. She rummaged in the case pretending to look for something.

"What have you lost? Anything I can lend you?"

"No thank you," said Lucy, her voice under the lid of the case.

"Why don't you unpack, then you'll be able to see where everything is?"

Lucy didn't answer.

"Buck up," Rachel urged, "and we'll go and lay siege to the boys."

"You go on without me," said Lucy. "I'll join you in a minute."

"But it would be more fun——" began Rachel, then shrugged. "Okay. Don't be long. I'll need all the support I can get." A few moments later Lucy could hear her hammering on the bathroom door. She got into her nightdress as quickly as she could. Then she stood for a moment taking deep breaths. "I'm alone," she said aloud to herself. "Alone. The next time may not be until I'm safely away."

After the battle of the bathroom, and a lot of thrown sponges, and bellowing upstairs from Uncle Peter they were at last all settled in bed and the lights out. It was strange to hear someone rustling and breathing so close in the dark. Lucy turned on her side, pressed the sheets over her ears.

"Lucy?" came Rachel's voice.

Lucy kept quite still.

"Lucy?" Rachel said again after a pause. "Are you asleep already?"

Stupid question. Lucy, longing to wriggle and with an unscratched tickle on her neck, began to ache from keeping still. Then at last Rachel breathed slowly and evenly. Lucy allowed herself to relax. The next best thing to being alone was being with someone who was asleep. In her mind she went over all the things that had happened since her arrival at this extraordinary household, and realised that not one of them—*not one of them*—had made a kind remark about Aunt Olive. Surely *somebody* could have said, "We're so sorry about your aunt." But they hadn't. Which just showed how little they truly cared. The realisation of this made her feel shrivelled inside.

The first shock next day was breakfast. At home it had been at exactly eight o'clock every morning. While Aunt Olive made the tea and toast and boiled the eggs, Lucy had laid the little table and they had listened to the radio (Thought for the Day and the Weather and then the News) while they ate. By nine o'clock everything was finished and cleared tidily away.

It was very different in this house. When Lucy woke with a jump it was to find Rachel was already dressed. She sat up in alarm. "Am I late?"

"Not a bit," Rachel said cheerfully. "There's nothing to be late *for* if you see what I mean."

"But breakfast——?"

"Oh, that. You don't have to worry about breakfast here. Everybody has it when they want to. I think the Old Folk have already had theirs."

Indeed, by the time the girls reached the kitchen, Uncle Peter and Aunt Gwen had already eaten and left the house. Bill was making himself a bowl of instant porridge. Patrick was chewing toast, his eyes on a book propped against the coffee-pot. The radio was on, but music came from it instead of news. With a shock of surprise Lucy realised it was half-past nine.

"Tea or coffee?" Rachel asked her.

Lucy asked for tea, was shown where the teapot lived, and left to make it. It was every man to his own toast, too, Patrick explained, waving his hand at a loaf by the toaster, and at once plunging back into 'Stereo and How it Works'. Lucy, having refused Rachel's offer to do her a fried egg with her own (horrid, even the *smell* of frying was nasty in the morning) organised her own breakfast and thought: they haven't the first idea how to look after a visitor.

"Where's Mum?" Rachel asked presently.

Patrick looked up from his book for only long enough to answer. "Shopping. And then she's got some committee or other. She's in a bit of a panic."

"Oh bother," said Rachel. "It looks as if I'd better do the ironing." She made a face towards a pile of garments on the washing-machine.

"I wouldn't," said Patrick, turning a page.

"No, you lazy brute. But I would."

"I should've warned Mum to hide it."

Rachel batted her brother on the head with an inside-out-newspaper, conveniently at hand.

"Well," he goaded, waving her away. "We don't want any more disasters." He avoided another blow and grinned at Lucy. "Last time she ironed she dropped the iron and blue sparks came out of it. The time before that she ruined a shirt. The time before that——"

"You shut up!" said Rachel. "At least I *try* to help!"

Lucy, struggling to choke down her toast, wished she could put her fingers in her ears. Yelling and fighting, jumping up and down, and all the time that

31

loud music—what a way to eat a meal! Bill finished his porridge and plumped himself down beside her. "Cheer up Lucy! Don't take any notice of *them!*" He jerked his head at his elder brother and sister. "They're at a difficult age!"

So are you, thought Lucy, saying nothing, and wishing she had never seen any of them.

At last breakfast came to a ragged end. Everyone washed up his own bits and pieces, Lucy noticed, though, there was a slight row over Bill's porridge pan. He claimed it would be better if left to soak. Rachel said thanks very much, she wasn't falling for *that* one, and Patrick joined in on her side. Bill gave in grudgingly, washed the pan but dashed out before anyone could make him dry it.

"Boys!" said Rachel, as she jerked the ironing board into position. Lucy watched her, amazed that anyone could iron so badly, and after a few minutes crept upstairs uncertain of what she ought to do. She re-made her bed slowly and carefully, then glanced at Rachel's, but decided she'd better not touch it. She would hate it if anybody interfered with *her* bed. She looked at her trunk and then at the waiting drawers but was more determined than ever to do nothing about that. She ought to be making plans to get away, she told herself, but somehow they were difficult to make. Not because it would have been hard to get away. Nobody in this house would have noticed whether she was in it, or not, let alone cared, but since last night's resolution, horrid doubts crept into her mind. Supposing she did find her way back to Church Road, what then? Would Mrs. Belling rush out with her arms spread and cry, "So glad to see you, duckie, we were hoping you'd come back?" No. Her kind face would pucker with worry and doubt, as she wondered what to do. "We'd best ask the Vicar," Lucy could hear her saying. And Mr. Thomas? He would look at her gravely and kindly, but he'd be disappointed. "I know you won't let us down, Lucy," he'd said.

She stared miserably round the room. Over the mantelpiece hung another picture of nothing. Just blue and red splotches and patches. As Lucy looked at the picture, the picture looked back. She hated it. She heard thundering footsteps on the stairs as the boys chased each other down. She hated them. She wondered where Aunt Gwen and Uncle Peter were, and what time they'd be back, and most of all how she was to endure life with these strange people. She hated them all.

She opened the trunk. Under the neatly folded clothes her fingers found the box holding the Chinese mother-of-pearl counters she and Aunt Olive used when playing whist or cribbage.

She spread the flat fish-shapes, wafer thin, on the bed. The pale winter sun winked on their delicate shimmering surfaces, green, gold, mauve, white. Lucy loved them because they were so exquisitely made—each scale and fin and round eye marked— and because they had once been part of a real sea-shell in which a creature had actually lived. Kneeling beside the bed, letting them lie coolly in her palms as she picked them up one by one, she remembered a summer evening when she had taken them into the garden and laid them out in patterns on the sun-warmed stone steps. It was a Sunday. The bells for evensong had been jangling away over the road. The garden was not large, but the corner where they sat was surrounded by old-fashioned roses: crimson, velvety and very sweet-smelling. Round the rose-bed was a stiff blue lavender hedge. Soon they would pick and dry the lavender to put into little purple muslin bags. They would turn some of the rose petals into pot-pourri. Meanwhile Aunt Olive sat knitting as Lucy played idly with the counters, and told her stories of long ago. Stories which her mother had told *her*, about horses and carriages, and lovely evening parties, and the clothes people wore. The sky turned to palest lemon, the sun caught Aunt Olive's twinkling silver knitting needles as her voice went quietly on . . .

The door burst open. Lucy was back in the chilly December bedroom. "Finished at last!" Rachel exclaimed, her arms stacked with folded garments. "What are you up to?"

"M-me?" Lucy stammered. Conscious of a flush, she tried to scrabble the counters together before Rachel had seen them.

But Rachel's eyes were quick. "What have you got there?" She dumped the ironing on her unmade bed so as to be able to see better.

"Nothing," Lucy mumbled. "Just some bits and pieces of mine."

Rachel sat, unasked, on Lucy's bed. "What are they?" She reached for one of the slender fish and examined it carefully, first one side then the other.

Lucy could have hit her. "Nothing special," she said in a tight voice, rattling the other counters into their box as quickly as she could.

Rachel was still staring at the fish, "What do you do with them?"

Lucy was sure Rachel would think it babyish if she answered "Play games with them," so instead she said, "You just keep them very carefully!" and twitched the little fish quickly from Rachel's palm.

Rachel's face, too, was suddenly red. "Well, there's no need to snatch! Did you think I was going to pinch it or something?"

34

They faced each other. In a funny sort of way Lucy did feel that Rachel taking an interest in Aunt Olive's fish was a sort of stealing. A spying, a prying. A robbing of something precious. But she could explain none of this so she stood panting a little, clutching the fish so tightly that its edge cut into her palm.

"If you think——" Rachel began, but Lucy never knew what she would have said, for at that moment there came a cheerful call from below. "Hello! Where's everybody?"

"Coming!" Rachel yelled back. Without a look at Lucy she grabbed up the pile of ironing and swept from the room.

Lucy's hands were damp, her breath coming in gasps as she shakily repacked the counters into the box and hid them at the very bottom of her trunk. She wished she had a key so that she could lock it. Then she heard a clamour of voices from below and among them Aunt Gwen's asking, "Where's Lucy?"

She hurried downstairs. Her aunt was distributing armfuls of shopping and directions to her family. "Bananas, chocolate biscuits, put them in the tin please, no *don't* eat them now—Bill you horrible child here are your jeans back from the cleaners. There's a note pinned on them to say they couldn't get all the stains out and I'm not surprised. Patrick, they say your shoes have gone past all mending. Ah, Lucy there you are! Look, I found some things for you. . . ." The things were a pair of denim dungarees and a bright red jersey, just Lucy's size. "I couldn't resist them," Aunt Gwen explained. "You'll spoil your nice clothes in this chaotic house I'm afraid, and anyway you'll feel more comfortable in these."

Lucy unwillingly took the brown paper parcel handed to her. She didn't want dungarees and jersey

35

that would make her look like her cousins, she wanted to look properly dressed. And she didn't want other people buying her clothes. But there was no time to protest, for almost at once Aunt Gwen rushed from the house again. "You've done the ironing? Rachel, you angel! Just organise the others into producing lunch, will you? There's ham, bake some potatoes, and here are the things for salad."

After she had gone, the four children worked together in the kitchen. Rachel was icily polite to Lucy, not meeting her eye as she handed her the things for the salad. The boys were less formal. Bill jostled cheerfully into her and she was hit on the cheek by a jet of water from the tap, which Patrick had intended for Bill. Both spluttered with laughter, and Patrick said, "Sorry Lucy. You got in the way."

Lucy pressed her lips together. It was so exactly what she had been thinking that she had to spend a long time dabbing at the front of her dress with the roller towel to hide her face. She was in the way here. And she'd be just as much in the way back at her old house or with Mr. Thomas or Mrs. Belling's family.

That was the trouble. She didn't belong anywhere.

Chapter Three

"But Dad," Patrick protested during lunch, "you must see that one of the attics would be the most fantastic place for a party."

"It wouldn't be so fantastic if the floor gave way underneath you all, would it?" said his father. "Do have some sense."

"All those trunks and things," said Bill. "I should think they must weigh more than we would."

"All those trunks and things don't clump about like your mob will."

"D'you mean dancing?" asked Rachel.

"You might call it dancing," said Uncle Peter. "I don't. But whatever it's called it's not going to happen in an attic, so I don't want to hear any more about it."

"A party downstairs wouldn't be the same," said Rachel wistfully.

"Don't have one then," said Aunt Gwen. "More ham, anybody?"

Sighs, and looks exchanged between the cousins, and between their parents. Lucy had no one to look at, and no one looked at her. She heaved a small sigh of her own.

"If you're really set on having it," Aunt Gwen

went on, as if there hadn't been any looks, "you'd better start planning it."

"What sort of planning?" Bill asked.

"A date and numbers would be a help," said his mother. "I'm sick and tired of trying to find out what you want. If you don't make up your mind soon there won't be time to ask anyone."

"But it doesn't take a minute to ask people," Rachel pointed out. "One morning on the telephone and it's done."

"You don't think it might be more polite to write to people?"

"Dear old Mum, quite mad," said Patrick kindly. "Nobody writes to anyone these days. Think of the cost of postage."

"Think of the telephone bills," said Uncle Peter.

"All right. We'll go and *see* people," said Rachel.

"Then do get on with it," urged Aunt Gwen. "If you leave it much longer it'll look so rude."

"But people are often asked to a party on the morning of them," Rachel pointed out. "Nobody minds a bit. Honestly, things are quite different from how it was in your young day."

Aunt Gwen smiled at Lucy. "You see they think I was born in the Ark and I expect you share their views. I'll leave you to sort things out between you."

The sorting out took place in one of the disputed attics. As soon as she entered it, Lucy had an odd sensation of familiarity—almost of welcome. An old sideboard, its face to the wall was rather like the one at The Shrubbery. There were two old trunks with curved lids and attached straps like Aunt Olive's which by now, filled with odd items would have been sold to strangers. But perhaps most of all it was the faint dusty fusty smell reminded her of the soft scents she was used to. For whatever reason, she felt

38

a curious lessening of her loneliness, and also that the attic was the only place in this house where she might be even a little happy.

Bill instantly scrambled on to the back of an old rocking horse in the corner. Its paint was battered and flaking, the tail missing, the bridle in tatters, but it was evident that Bill was fond of it. "Good old Pegasus," he said affectionately, patting the place where the mane should have been, and rocking with energy. For the first time, Lucy felt she might almost be able to like Bill.

"Is he—was he—yours?" she asked him.

"No. Worse luck. I wish he had been. I could have done with him when I was younger. It was one of the things in the attic when we got here. There was quite a lot of stuff that's been up here years."

"Like this trunk," said Patrick, sitting on one. "Now about this party——"

"But whose are they?" Lucy couldn't help asking.

"We don't know," Rachel told her. "Not the people who were here before us. They were ancient, and they said they'd bought them with the house. We haven't even opened the trunks, so goodness knows——"

"Rachel, do stop gossiping," urged Patrick, "or we'll never get organised."

"Sorry. Yes. But I wanted to tell Lucy——"

"Tell her later. Bill, stop messing about on that horse, and concentrate. We'll make a list of who we'd each like to ask, and then——"

Lucy's mind was far away. What extraordinary people! To have bought by lucky accident these mysterious old trunks, and not even have bothered to look inside! They might be full of *treasure*, for all they knew. And here they were, just using them to sit on! It was probably because the trunks were old that they despised them. Typical. When they could be bothered, they'd probably burn them. Unopened. So that Uncle Peter could fill this dear old attic with fitted cupboards and ugly pictures. . . .

". . . And how about you, Lucy?" Rachel was asking.

She jumped. All three of them were looking at her expectantly. "Er—um—I'm sorry, I didn't hear what you were saying," she mumbled.

Bill began a big sigh, Rachel flashed him a warning glance which Lucy saw, and said patiently, "We were asking how many friends you'd like to ask to the party?"

"Me?" said Lucy. "None. At least—it's not my party, is it? It's yours."

"It's ours," Rachel corrected her. "Of course while you're living here you'll join in everything, so the party's as much yours as ours so you must ask your friends to it."

Patrick was holding a biro over a scribbling block on which a long list of names was already written. He was clearly waiting for more. Panic filled Lucy. She had no friends. And even if she had, she wouldn't want to ask them to any parties given by the cousins. In any case, by the time it was given she hoped to be somewhere else, far away.

Patrick said, "Honestly Lucy, we'd love to meet your friends. Just tell us who they are and we'll give them a ring. Unless they're too far away, that is."

She seized gratefully on the excuse. "I'm afraid they are."

Rachel said, "Don't let that worry you too much if it's only a few. Mum's very good about people staying overnight, especially if they bring their own sleeping bags."

Lucy, who knew only vaguely what a sleeping bag

was and associated it with camping, shook her head. "Thank you, but I don't think it would be worth trying."

Rachel looked doubtfully at Patrick, who said, "What, nobody?"

Lucy stared down at her hands. "I don't think so. Thank you." Although she was not looking their way she could feel their glances at each other. She tried desperately to think of a satisfactory excuse. Just as she had decided there was none, and that she had no choice but to explain the truth, an idea came to her. From nowhere, it seemed. "Just at the moment," she murmured, in a rather special sort of voice, "I'd rather not meet anyone from where I used to live."

As soon as she had said it she went hot all over. Aunt Olive had always said, "Tell the truth and shame the devil." What she had just said had been a particularly nasty sort of lie. She met nobody's eye.

"O.K.," Rachel said quickly. "We quite understand. If you're sure." More meaning glances. Then further talk about the party. This time Lucy listened. She was amazed at what she heard. This affair was not going to be a *party* at all! Lucy knew about parties, for Aunt Olive had often described them: everybody in their prettiest clothes. Games, sometimes with prizes to be won. Gorgeous food, sandwiches and trifles and jellies. Sometimes dancing. Often a present to take home at the end.

But the gathering the cousins were now describing was quite different. People weren't even expected to arrive until eight o'clock. It was hoped that some would bring records to play. There was to be no proper party food, just crisps and nuts. Coke and fruit cup to drink. No games at all. What was everyone going to *do*? Apparently stand about and talk. This dreary programme was to end at midnight.

41

"That seems to be the lot," said Patrick, "unless anyone has any other ideas?"

Lucy sensed that the girl in the corner wanted to say something. What girl? There were only four of them; herself and the three cousins. Lucy laughed silently at herself. Soon she'd need glasses! But from the side of her eye the dust-sheet draped across an old armchair had looked extraordinarily like the pale dress of some one sitting in it.

"Sure, Lucy?" Patrick asked, bringing her back to her proper self. "Right. Then we can tell Mum everything's settled."

They all shuffled out of the attic. As they left, Lucy gave it a last lingering look. "I'll be back," she promised it. "As soon as I get the chance."

The chance came next morning when the cousins decided to visit as many of their friends as possible to ask them to the party. They took it for granted that Lucy would be going with them till she said she would rather not. "I don't know any of them, you see."

"But you could get to know them before the party," Patrick pointed out, "if you come with us."

"It's all right, thank you." She set her mouth in a firm line. They hesitated. Then Rachel said, "If that's the way you want it." They set off without her.

Aunt Gwen was surprised and not pleased to find her left behind.

"I didn't want to go, honestly," said Lucy. "I—I want to write a letter." Another lie, but she could make that one right by writing to Mrs. Belling. She'd said she would.

Aunt Gwen looked at her searchingly. "Are you sure?"

"Quite sure," said Lucy in her most decided voice. She moved towards the stairs. Aunt Gwen went into the study. Lucy deliberately pausing, heard her say in a worried way. "Pete, I'm not sure the children are doing everything that they might to———" The study door clicked shut. Lucy went on upstairs, but instead of turning in at Rachel's bedroom she continued up to the attic. The stuffy half-familiar smell met her as she opened the door. When she had shut it she felt safe at last. No one would think of looking for her here.

As soon as she began to explore, she was glad she had grudgingly put on the new jeans and jersey. She wouldn't have wanted her own clothes to have brushed against the dusty trunks and furniture. Old-fashioned pictures were stacked against the wall. She moved one, then another, admiring them. The third frame, a heavy gold one, held not a picture but a mirror. Lucy crouched to peer into its mottled surface. Her own pale face peered back at her. And then, suddenly, there was another face beside it, a round laughing one. Lucy turned swiftly in surprise and alarm.

"Aha!" said the girl, her dark eyes sparkling. "At last!"

Lucy stared. The girl wore an oddly long dress, a pinafore, short boots ... and an expression of sly triumph.

"Who—who are you?" Lucy stammered. "Where did you come from?"

"I'm Alice," said the girl, "and I live here. The question is—who are *you*?"

*　　*　　*

Patrick, Rachel and Bill sauntered down the road. Eight houses had been called at, five of them successfully. Twelve guests had accepted with enthusiasm, two had to wait for parental approval, one had refused (another party the same day). Now there was a patch of walking to be done before they reached the next area to be visited. It was Bill who said into a silence, "Well, what do you think of her?"

"Give her a chance, she's only just arrived," said Rachel.

"It seems to me," said Bill, "she's been here for ever."

"Oh, come on," said Patrick. "She's not so bad. Mousey, but then she's probably terrified out of her wits."

"Yes," Rachel agreed. "Remember she's been living all alone in an old house with an ancient aunt all her life. We must be an enormous change."

"But surely a change for the better?" said Bill. "Being shut up with the aunt must have been ghastly."

"Mum said she liked it," said Rachel.

"How does she know?"

"She had a long talk on the telephone with the Vicar who lived next door. He told her a lot of things, and she passed some of them on to me."

"Why only some and only you?" said Bill. "Why not all the things and all of us?"

"Poor old Rachel's bound to see more of her," Patrick pointed out. "And Mum did explain that she'd never been to school or anything and was bound to be a bit different from most people."

"Yes I'd forgotten that. No school. Ever. Lucky animal," said Bill.

"Lucky?" said Patrick. "The aunt taught her."

"Correction. Unlucky. Why?"

Rachel shrugged. "I'm not sure. Perhaps she was delicate or something."

"I think," said Rachel, "from things Mum said—

or rather *didn't* say—that the aunt was a bit eccentric."

"Eccentric?" echoed Bill. "You mean 'nuts'?"

"No I don't. It's odd, unusual—What exactly *does* eccentric mean, Patrick?"

"Er—um, let's see. Ec-centric. A bit off-centre."

"What I thought: nuts," said Bill. "Poor old Lucy. Perhaps it was catching."

"Oh—*Bill*——!"

"But just look at the way she never says anything. Or *does* anything, just sits about and looks weedy."

"Bill, you're not being fair," Rachel's voice was severe. "That aunt, even if she was awful, was all she had instead of parents. How would you feel if Mum and Dad suddenly weren't there any more?"

"I can't think," said Bill, after trying to imagine for a few moments.

"Exactly. So you see," said Rachel. "We've got to make allowances like the Old Folk said."

"We keep making them all the time." Bill sounded aggrieved. "She doesn't seem to notice."

"She doesn't seem pleased about anything," Rachel admitted.

"Perhaps she isn't," suggested Patrick simply. "We're used to us, but she isn't. Perhaps she hates the lot of us."

"Then *she* hasn't given *us* a chance," Bill pointed out. "She might at least have come out this morning."

"What would happen to her if she didn't stay with us?" Rachel asked Patrick.

"I don't know. Dad said there really wasn't anywhere else for her to be."

"Poor, poor thing!" exclaimed Rachel. "If she really hasn't anyone else——"

"Apparently not. Dad said if he and Mum had

45

known about Lucy when she was orphaned, they might have offered to adopt her."

"Gosh!" Bill was astounded by this idea.

"Very decent of the Old Folk even to think of it," Patrick agreed; then added honestly. "I'm glad they didn't."

"So am I," Bill agreed with fervour. "Just think. *I* might never have happened if they had."

Patrick looked sideways at his brother. "And there are days, young Bill, when I can think of advantages which——"

Bill aimed a kick, Patrick leapt aside to avoid it. Rachel had been thinking. "It might have been better if they had. Then we could have brought her up properly."

"True. She might have turned out better then," Patrick agreed.

"She couldn't have turned out worse," said Bill gloomily.

*   *   *

"I'm Lucy," said Lucy.

"You don't look like a Lucy. You look more like a boy."

Lucy looked down in shame at her jeans. "Oh these. They're not the sort of things I usually wear."

"No, you had proper clothes the first day," Alice agreed.

"How do you know?" asked Lucy quickly. "I've never seen you before."

Alice smiled. "But I saw you."

"Where?"

"You'd be surprised. Now do stop asking questions and——"

But Lucy had time to stare wildly round the attic. The old furniture, the pictures, the rocking horse,

trunks, had disappeared. In their place was a neat
iron bed, a chair, a white painted chest of drawers.
"Where am I?" she cried.

"With me, in Flo's bedroom. Quite safe. But do
hush or someone'll hear you——"

"Yes. Rachel might," said Lucy, forgetting Rachel
was out.

"Who's Rachel? That girl?" Alice looked suddenly less friendly.

"Yes. My cousin. She lives here."

"She doesn't. *I* live here. With Mademoiselle. No
one else at present. Except the servants, of course."

"But——" There were a thousand questions Lucy
wanted to ask. Or *had* wanted to ask. For a curious
sensation, rather like pins and needles in the brain,
if such a thing were possible, was becoming stronger
and stronger. Already it had blurred her first shock
of astonishment. Now, though still confused, she
found she could not remember the important things
she wanted to know. Like—who was Alice? What
happened to the attic? And how? And why? . . .
why? . . . The pins and needles sharpened.

"There's no need to be frightened," said Alice,
taking her hand. "You've chosen a good day to come.
Mama and Papa are away and Mademoiselle has
gone out. We can watch for her from the window.
When we see her you can escape down the back
stairs. Just like a story!" Impetuously she started to
pull Lucy across the room.

"Wait a minute—I don't understand——"

But Alice would not let her wait. "We'll talk in
the school-room, it's warmer there, and anyway you
can't stay here. Flo might come up."

Still dazed, Lucy allowed herself to be towed out
of the room and down the stairs. These, at any rate,
seemed much the same as usual: dark, winding and

uncarpeted. But the landing was quite different from how Lucy—now very distantly—remembered it. The walls which a few minutes ago had been bare but for one or two peculiar pictures were now a riot of pattern blossoms over a trellis. The window was looped with heavy velvet curtains, a chaise-longue stood before it. Alice went ahead into the spare room—only it wasn't the spare room. A fire burned in the little black grate, there was a big table, several chairs, a patterned screen, and in the corner——

"Pegasus!" Lucy exclaimed. "But just now it was——"

"Dobbin. He's beautiful, isn't he?" said Alice, gratified by Lucy's admiration. "You can have a turn on him presently if you like. But first tell me all about yourself. I've waited so long for you to come!"

"But you—I—" Lucy was becoming more and more lost. "I don't understand——"

"Don't bother about understanding!" said Alice impatiently. "I can understand enough for both of us. Just tell me things. This house is your home now?"

"No." Even in the muzziness following the pins and needles, Lucy was sure of that. "This isn't my *home*. That was—" Faintly, like a blurred photograph, she saw a memory of The Shrubbery "—another house. . ."

"Yes?" Alice prompted.

It was almost impossible to remember. There'd been a kind person—"With my Aunt Olive," Lucy managed suddenly. "And then . . . and then . . . she died. So I had to come here."

"When are you going away again?"

"I don't know. Perhaps never, they said——"

Alice gave a sigh of satisfaction. "Good. That's

48

what I wanted to know. So this *is* your home now. You'll always be here——"

"No—!" Lucy protested, but without energy. Her memories were too hazy, the problem too far away to matter much. Far more important and immediate was Alice, the newly-painted rocking horse, the comfortable schoolroom. So instead of trying to convince her strange new companion any longer, she only said, "Oh very well. If you don't believe me, I don't care."

"Good," said Alice. "I don't want to waste time with quarrelling. I hardly ever have anyone to play with."

"Haven't you any brothers or sisters?"

"Yes, six, but all much older. My three sisters have all married and gone away and my oldest brother is in the army in India and the other two are at boarding school. Mama and Papa go away a great deal as well, so that often leaves just Mademoiselle and me."

"Mademoiselle!" said Lucy remembering her. "When will she be back?"

"Don't worry, not for a long time. She says she has to walk across the common to fetch medicine for her cough, but *I* know that she has a gentleman friend. They meet and walk up and down together, talking."

"How do you know?"

"Because once I happened to be outside the door of the maids' hall when Mabel was saying something to Flo about it. So next time Mademoiselle went out, I slipped out too and followed her."

"Alice, that was spying!" Lucy was shocked. "And listening at doors."

"Sometimes," said Alice, a determined look coming to her face, "you have to do that kind of thing just to get your own way. Surely you know that by

49

now? Now do stop worrying about Mademoiselle. Let's play something. Do you know any games?"

"Of course."

"Then come to the toy cupboard and we'll choose one."

The cupboard was full of entrancing things:—a chess set, dominoes, several wax dolls, fish-shaped counters which made Lucy gasp with half-puzzled recognition, a pack of 'Happy Family' cards. . . . She could willingly have spent the rest of the morning delving among such treasures, but Alice was impatient to play something. She took a set of slender ivory sticks from the shelf. "Can you play spillikins?"

"Of course," said Lucy, and half an hour later, Alice had to admit that she could indeed play spillikins well, for Lucy had beaten her soundly.

"I'll set them up again. Your turn."

It was half way through this game that Alice's hand shook so much that the whole pile toppled.

"Bad luck," said Lucy.

"Luck? You nudged me!"

"I didn't."

"You did. With your elbow. Quite hard. I'll have to have that turn again."

"But I didn't—you can't—"

Alice's face was red and angry. "You may not have felt it, but you did. Now stop talking while I have my proper turn."

"It's not your turn, it's mine!" But Alice was already picking at the pile of spilled sticks. Lucy closed her mouth and said nothing till the game was ended.

"There!" Alice cried. "I knew I'd win! I always beat Mademoiselle." Her eyes flashed with triumph.

"You didn't win, because you cheated," said Lucy. "So it doesn't count."

"How dare you!" Alice actually stamped a booted foot. "You're being perfectly hateful!"

Lucy stood up suddenly. "I don't think I want to play with you any more."

"And *I* don't want to play with *you*." For a moment they faced each other flushed and angry. Then Alice quickly put her hand on Lucy's arm. "Don't let's quarrel."

"I wasn't quarrelling," said Lucy stiffly.

"You were. We both were. Such a waste. I do so want us to be friends."

And in spite of Alice's obvious cheating, Lucy knew that she wanted to be friends as well. Perhaps it was because of this, or perhaps it was the soothing atmosphere in the cosy firelit schoolroom, but suddenly anger died in her. "So do I," she said. "Perhaps I did nudge you a bit. I can't remember."

Alice was already putting away the spillikins. "Would you like to look at my scrapbook?"

"I'd love to," said Lucy, first because this was true, then because mention of a scrapbook was reassuring and comfortable.

She and Aunt Olive had spent many winter evenings cutting out pictures from old Christmas cards and magazines to make the scrapbooks for children in hospital. Alice's was a much more beautiful one than either of theirs had been though. Large, heavy and leather bound with thick stiff pages. They put it on the worn hearthrug and lay on their fronts on the floor to see it better. All the pictures were old-fashioned but Lucy loved them the better for that. Under each was a title written in Alice's small clear hand. Soon the only sound was the slow swishing of the leaves as they turned and Alice's voice explaining each page. The fire flickered and faded. Comfort stole more deeply into the room. Lucy had quite forgotten that she had ever belonged anywhere else. The two girls became so engrossed in the scrapbook that when voices were suddenly heard downstairs it was a shock to both of them.

"Mademoiselle!" cried Alice leaping up, her eyes wide. "Quick! She mustn't see you! Up to Flo's room again! It's the only safe place. Hurry!"

They let themselves quietly out of the schoolroom and sped along the landing. At the foot of the attic stairs Alice snatched urgently at Lucy's arm. "You'll come again, won't you?"

"If I can," said Lucy, meaning it.

"Promise?"

"I can't promise. Let me go."

Alice's grip tightened. "Not till you've promised. *And* not to tell anyone else about me. Ever."

"I can't——"

"Aleece? Aleece?" called a voice.

"Mademoiselle! Promise—or she'll find you."

"You don't want her to," Lucy pointed out, but she herself did not want to be discovered. She twitched her arm from Alice's grasp and fled up the narrow dark stairs. After her came Alice's voice. "Promise! Promise!"

Lucy let herself into Flo's bedroom, panting. She must get away. But how? She couldn't think properly. It was as if her inside mind refused to work for her. As though it didn't belong to her. As if she wasn't herself at all. Was she?

To make certain she was she glanced into Flo's mirror. Reassuringly, the face that stared back, though wide-eyed and pale, was undoubtedly her own. Her faint sigh of relief caught in mid-breath. For something else had also caught her eye in the glass: the chipped and battered face of Dobbin—no, of Pegasus. She swung round. Seeing the junk-filled attic again brought back her breath in jerky gasps. There was the trunk on which Patrick had sat. Shakily, she put out a hand towards the rocking horse. Yes, the shiny newness was long gone. He was bald, shabby, old.

"Dobbin?" Lucy whispered. "Pegasus? Where have we been?"

His painted eye met hers, knowing, guarded. Lucy felt as she had after she had once had flu. Muzzy and tremulous.

A voice floated up from the landing below, a voice that was calling. Her first reaction was: "Mademoiselle! She's coming up after me!"

Then she knew the voice to be Rachel's and the words to be, "Lucy, Lucy where are you? It's lunch time!"

Chapter Four

LUCY spent the rest of the day in a bewildered state. Had it really happened? Or had she simply fallen asleep for a few moments beside the mirror? She would have liked to believe that that was the right explanation, because it was the simplest. Any other idea was too fantastic to be considered seriously. And yet, and yet. . .

Alice had been so real. She could see her vividly in her mind's eye now, and hear her shrill imperious little voice. It was because she was trying so hard to remember some of the things that Alice had said, that other voices didn't penetrate her consciousness.

"You're half asleep, Lucy!" Uncle Peter teased her during lunch. "Did you have a bad night?"

Lucy flushed. "No. Fine, thank you."

Aunt Gwen raised an eyebrow at Rachel.

"No," said Rachel, "we *didn't* talk till all hours!"

Lucy shook her head. That was one thing she was sure of. She and Rachel had not talked at all. Probably they never would. Yet had it been Alice in that other bed, there would have been plenty to chatter about. For already Lucy felt she knew Alice better than she would ever know Rachel. Strange, that. Perhaps it was because Alice so evidently wanted the company, while Rachel pretended to be friendly only because it was her duty.

Later, Aunt Gwen, sailing into the kitchen with a vase of tattered chrysanthemums, found Lucy alone. She began to pluck the dead flowers one by one from the vase. "Are you beginning to feel a bit more settled in with us yet?"

Lucy longed to escape but was not sure how to. She fidgeted her feet, watching Aunt Gwen refill the vase and start to arrange fresh chrysanthemums she'd bought that morning. Stab—stab—stab went the stiff stalks into the vase, and amazingly stayed where they'd been placed. Neither she herself nor Aunt Olive had been able to make tall flowers do what they were told like that. They'd stuck more safely to small mixed posies. She sighed now as she thought of them.

Aunt Gwen, her eyes on the chrysanthemums, said, "I do hope you soon will. I expect you found this a terribly rackety household at first, but let's hope you'll get used to it." She smiled at Lucy. She had a very warm smile that used up all of her face. Lucy only just managed to stop herself smiling back. It wouldn't do to let Aunt Gwen think the two of them were going to be friends when they were not. She now snapped a stem short, slit the end of it and with one of her fast, apparently careless movements placed it exactly where she wanted it. The chrysanthemums were taking on a fan-shape, all their faces looking frontwards. Lucy had to admit to herself the effect was rather splendid.

"Are you fond of doing flowers?"

"No," said Lucy promptly, but because that was not strictly true added, "at least, not like that. Only little mixed-up bunches."

"And very charming they can be," said Aunt

Gwen, "only this is a difficult time of year for them. Spring's better. You must do some for us then." She smiled again. Lucy looked at the floor. She wouldn't be here in the spring.

"There!" said Aunt Gwen briskly, sticking in the last flower and standing back to judge the arrangement. "That's finished I think, do you? Now I must go and write some letters. You will let me know, won't you, if there's anything particular you'd like to do this holiday? I'm sure we could arrange it."

"Yes. Thank you." Lucy had a sudden idea. "There is one thing. You know about arty sort of things, don't you?"

Aunt Gwen smiled. "Like what?"

"Historical costumes? Have you got any books about them with pictures in?"

Aunt Gwen looked surprised. "Yes. Somewhere. Why?"

"Could I look at them?"

"Of course. If you're interested." Her aunt looked pleased. "Any particular place or period?"

"England." That was easy. But period? "About —about—I'm not sure." Lucy realised with dismay how little history she actually knew. She made a guess. "Victorian times, perhaps. And who came after her?"

"Edward the Seventh. Hour-glass figures and leg-of-mutton sleeves, and boaters. Agony to wear I should think, but most attractive."

"Yes. Well. Do you think I could see the books now?"

"This minute, you mean?"

Lucy hid her eagerness beneath politeness. "If that wouldn't be too much trouble."

"I'm not sure that I know exactly——" Aunt Gwen began. Then she saw Lucy's face. "But I'm

56

sure we can find them between us." She gathered the dead flowers into a basket and handed it to Lucy. "Shove these in the dustbin, will you? I'll put this vase in the hall, then we'll look in the study and see what we can find."

Because the family's books had not been properly sorted since the move, it took a long time to find the right ones. But at last Lucy found herself with an armful which Aunt Gwen said she might enjoy. "But why the special interest?" she asked curiously.

Lucy hesitated. Aunt Gwen seemed a kind person, but to try to explain the extraordinary adventure of the morning would be quite out of the question. She'd think Lucy was mad, or making it up. Probably both. "Because—because——" All at once she knew what she could say. "We were doing this bit in history lessons, when——" She stopped deliberately. "I'd rather not talk about it," she ended in a pathetic voice.

She was filled with hot shame when she saw Aunt Gwen's swift understanding look. Why had she said that?

"Then of course you'll want to go on with what you were doing," Aunt Gwen sounded very matter-of-fact. "But don't spend too long working, will you? You're supposed to be on holiday now, and I know the children have got plans. . . ."

"Yes. Of course," agreed Lucy backing towards the door with her load. She could not wait to get away, less because she was impatient to examine the books than because of her aunt's unspoken sympathy made her hate herself.

Once upstairs—thank goodness Rachel wasn't about—Lucy tried to put Aunt Gwen out of her mind. This was not too difficult because searching pictures was as exciting as a treasure hunt. A difficult one, though, for though the books had a number of pictures of ladies and gentlemen there were not so many of children. And she'd seen no grown-ups this morning. Then she found a whole section on children's clothes. She flipped through the pages. Little boys with hoops, girls with white frilly drawers hanging below their skirts, and bonnets. No. . . . A girl wearing a frock with a huge bell-shaped skirt, just like her mother beside her, no. She turned several pages impatiently. Now boys and girls were in sailor suits, black stockings and buttoned boots. Still wrong. She turned back. Ah! This was more like it. . . . And this. . . And there, suddenly, was Alice! The frilled petticoat over the dress, curiously bunched up behind. The hair scooped up into a ribbon and worn loose. It could have *been* Alice. Lucy looked swiftly at the date under the illustration. 1873. A hundred years ago!

She turned to the last book. The author of this one had been as interested in furniture as in clothes. Many of the illustrations were of rooms. Now that she knew what she was looking for, it was easy for Lucy to turn to the right section. 'A typical late Victorian Drawing-room', she read, and saw several ladies standing about in stiff long dresses, straight in front but looped into large decorated loops behind. "Bustles," murmured Lucy wisely to herself, already feeling quite knowledgeable from what she had read. So that's what Alice's Mama would have looked like. And the drawing-room—why it was just like the photographs in Aunt Olive's album—the same clutter of little tables, loaded with ornaments, chairs at every angle, the piano, the crowded mantelshelf, the tasselled bell-pulls each side of it. . .

"What ever are you doing?" Rachel appeared suddenly.

"Reading," said Lucy defensively. "Your mother lent me some books."

"But reading up here? You must be frozen!"

Lucy found she was indeed cold. And stiff. "Yes, well——"

Rachel was looking at one of the books. "'A Social History of England in the Nineteenth Century'," she read from the spine. "History!" she repeated in amazement.

"History can be very interesting," said Lucy.

"Rather you than me. Look, there's a science-fiction serial on the box. Quite dotty but good fun. Would you like to come and watch?"

Lucy went with her. It was easier to do what these people expected, and anyhow she was quite pleased to see television, whatever the programme. But, as was only to be expected, the episode had hardly begun before a quarrel broke out.

Patrick, who had been muttering under his breath since the beginning suddenly exploded at the sight of a robot. "A man dressed up in tin boxes, nuts and bolts and a flashing light! How unconvincing can you *get*? The whole story's nonsense, if you ask me."

"We didn't, and it is, but it doesn't really matter. You're liking it really," said Bill.

"I don't understand a word," Patrick contradicted.

"That's because you didn't watch last week. Everything's peculiar because they're a thousand years on in the future."

"I'd like to know how they managed that, for a start."

"Oh do shut up," said Rachel. "Either watch it or go away."

"I bet you don't understand it either."

"I do. They found a time machine last week. Only

they're not quite sure how it works, so they keep landing up at odd times when they don't expect to."

"They sound pretty dim——"

"Do be *quiet*."

"Oh all *right*!" Patrick slumped in his chair, pretending to be bored, but watching the rest of the programme through half-closed eyes. As soon as it was over, he returned to the attack. "Why can't they put on a decent scientific documentary instead of this stuff? Something that really tells you about going through time."

"But can you? Really?" asked Bill, eyes round.

"Of course not," said Rachel.

"How do you know?" Patrick demanded. "The scientists in America and Russia and places are always streaks ahead of anything we knew. Have been for years. Once they've discovered the trick of how to do it, travelling into another century will be as common as taking a bus down the High Street."

"Oh Patrick, I do hope you're right!" Rachel clasped her knees. "I'm not too keen about the future, but there are so many times in the past I'd like a look at——" She nudged Lucy. "Where would you start?"

But Lucy's inside mind had already slid away from them. 'The trick of how to do it' was what she must find out. Once she'd mastered that, perhaps she'd be able to sort out the rest. Because before she left, she must. It would be too tantalising never to know who Alice had been. And besides, she'd like to see her again, just once. . .

"——or perhaps Cleopatra? I'd love a good gossip with her," Rachel was saying. Lucy looked at her blankly. As always, once she began to think about Alice, the others seemed to fade away, become less important. Less obtrusive. She had already forgotten what they had been talking about before she had begun to concentrate on her own problems.

"Do wake *up*, Lucy!" Bill sounded exasperated. Rachel gave him a sisterly look. Patrick aimed a swipe at his bottom. "But she's never *with* us!" Bill protested as if indeed Lucy weren't present.

"I was thinking," she said with dignity.

"Which is something some of us haven't learned to do yet," Patrick said.

Bill hurled a cushion. Patrick hurled it back. Rachel threw herself between them.

Lucy crept from the room.

*   *   *

A few minutes later, Aunt Gwen came through the house, as Patrick put it, 'like a whirlwind'.

"Pete! Pete! It's *Tuesday*! The day of the Gardiners' party! How could I have forgotten?"

The family gathered in a rush.

"The wonder is that you remembered in time. I suppose it *is* in time?" Patrick enquired.

Aunt Gwen looked wildly at the clock. "Just about. Pete, give me ten minutes. Fifteen."

"You can have the whole night as far as I'm concerned," said Uncle Peter, strolling out of his study. "I don't want to spend it talking to Fred Gardiner and his horrible friends. Let's not bother."

But Aunt Gwen was sure they should. Mrs. Gardiner, she said, would notice and be hurt if they weren't there.

"That seems to settle that then," said Uncle Peter with resignation. He turned to Patrick. "What will you lot do?"

Patrick grinned at his father. "Grub up some pitiful little supper, I suppose. Think about us as you

61

stuff yourself with party food, making do with the odd crust——"

"Watch it," his father warned. "You'll have her up in the air again."

Aunt Gwen was up in the air already. "Crusts! I forgot to get in any bread!"

Bill turned to Patrick. "It's awful isn't it? We ought to be in care, really."

Patrick nodded. "The 1970's. Father in work, mother ablebodied. And here we are, starving."

"Like poor unwanted little orphans," said Bill.

There was a moment of embarrassed silence. Nobody looked at Lucy. Then Rachel said quickly. "You do talk rubbish, you boys! Why don't you look up a decent film and we can have fish and chips afterwards? Come on Mum, I'll be your lady's maid. Lucy, you'd better come too. She needs all the help she can get."

Lucy was swept upstairs to her aunt's bedroom. Aunt Olive would have been horribly shocked at the state it was in. Clothes were flung everywhere. One evening sandal proved lost and had to be hunted for in the depths of an untidy cupboard. Aunt Gwen whisked about, taking off make-up, kicking off her shoes, banging drawers open and shut, all the time giving breathless instructions to herself and the girls. "—Which dress, long or short? Long I think. Rachel, the green one—Lucy, be an angel and see if there's a gold evening bag on the top shelf—thank you, Rachel, now the cloak—heavens, I hope I sewed its button on—no, here it is—needle and thread, quick!—now put the things out of *this* bag into that—now, where's my brush——?"

Thanks to frantic efforts of Lucy and Rachel, she was ready in exactly fourteen and a half minutes. Patrick had timed her. She swept down the stairs, her black velvet cloak swishing behind her, looking, Lucy thought, really rather beautiful in her strange way. Uncle Peter waited patiently while she fired off a last minute salvo of questions. "Have you found a film? Which picture house? Have you got a key, Patrick? What time shall we be back, Pete?"

"Search me," said Uncle Peter, "I haven't even seen the invitation."

"I don't think there was one. She rang up."

"Aha!" Patrick was quick to pounce. "What's all this about good manners and proper parties, then?" He raised his eyebrows at Lucy. "No wonder there's a galloping generation gap. Talk about not practising what you preach! Do stop fussing, Mum, and get going or the party'll be over before you've arrived. What's the matter now?"

"I said, have you found a decent film?"

"No, a very indecent one. Labelled XXX for adults over seventy-five only. But don't worry, Bill and I are going to put on false beards and the girls will wear white wigs and shawls and by the time we get back we'll know all sorts of terrible things you don't think we ought to know which of course we know already anyway, and——"

"Patrick, do be sensible! Pete, make him behave. What is it really?"

Uncle Peter took her arm. "Calm yourself. It's a highly respectable spy film."

"Wholesome family entertainment," Bill put in.

"It's half-rate for pensioners on Monday. You two had better go on Monday," said Patrick, "and don't ask if we've got supper money, because we have, and don't say come straight home, because we will, and *do* have a good time!"

Uncle Peter hustled Aunt Gwen off while she was

63

still protesting wildly about switching off lights and not talking to strangers.

"That's them launched on their orgy," said Patrick as the car drove away. "Now for us. We've got ten minutes."

There was a rush upstairs. Lucy, of course, was part of it though no one she noticed had bothered to ask her if she wanted to go to a film or not. As a matter of fact the idea of going out at night without any grown-ups was exciting and the film was even more so, but she was not going to admit this even to herself.

Because it was an occasion she put on Aunt Olive's new coat for the first time.

"Hey!" cried Bill, as soon as he saw her. "You can't go to the Regal in that get up!"

"Honestly not." Rachel agreed. "It's an awful flea-pit, and just think of the fish and chip dribble! Put on your jeans. Much more sensible, and you'll look just like us."

Lucy scowled. The last thing she wanted was to look like *them*. But with Rachel so sure and Patrick muttering, "If you're going to change, do get *on* with it!" there seemed no escape.

It seemed strange to be out at night in those peculiar clothes with no grown-up in charge. Her cousins took the matter entirely for granted. Evidently they were allowed to wander about when and where looking as dreadful as they chose. Lucy was self-conscious on the bus. What must people think of them? It did not occur to her to notice that there were more young people dressed like she was now than like she used to be in Aunt Olive's time. Certainly no one seemed to take any notice.

The film was most exciting, quite unlike any that Lucy had seen before. In the interval Bill rushed off to queue for icecreams and orangeade in cartons for them all. Again Lucy, who had been taught never to eat or drink in a public place, was embarrassed. If Aunt Olive could see her now! When the programme was over they jostled into the crisp night with the rest of the crowd. Patrick made a joke about the film. Bill and Rachel laughed. A woman waiting at a nearby bus stop gave them a disapproving glare and turned to say something to her friend. She thinks we were laughing at her, thought Lucy. She feels just like Aunt Olive and I used to feel. She felt sorry for the woman.

The windows of the fish and chip shop threw orange squares of light on to the pavement. They joined the queue already formed. A strong smell of frying floated out from the steamy interior.

"I'm starving!" Bill announced loudly, rubbing his tummy. Let's all have double portions. Can we? Is there enough money?"

"Greedy hog," said Patrick. "But there is."

"Good," said Bill. "It's all that suspense. It tires you out and being tired uses up energy and any energy needs replacing by good food. So it's not my fault I'm starving, it's the film's."

"Four double portions," ordered Patrick when it was their turn. "Salt and vinegar on all of them—oh, Lucy, salt and vinegar for you?"

"Er—no. Thank you." Fish and chips would be bad enough she thought without other things splashed on to them.

But in fact they were delicious. She was amazed. Perhaps—if one could put Aunt Olive right out of one's mind—there was something rather special about wandering about the lamplit streets eating out of a paper bag. The chips were hot, the fish crumbled and the juice ran down to her elbow.

(They'd been right about not wearing her coat.) This is rather fun, Lucy caught herself thinking, and immediately felt guilty. It might be fun but it was a disgraceful way to behave.

The bus slid up to them. Hurriedly, greasy paper bags were scrumpled and put in the litter bin. The party leaped on board the bus and swayed off into the night.

Later in bed, Lucy realised that a whole day had gone by with no plans made for running away. She'd hardly ever thought about it. Tomorrow she really would. But first she must solve the mystery of Alice.

Chapter Five

FOR once, everyone was present, if sleepy, at the breakfast table next morning.

"Have a good orgy?" Patrick enquired cheerfully.

His father scowled at him from over the newspaper. "Ice-cold room, tiny cocktail eats, and everyone wanting free advice on the side. If you call that a good orgy, yes."

"It wasn't as bad as all that," said Aunt Gwen. "I met a man who was interested in housing. I think I might scrape him on to one of my committees."

"Of course if everyone you meet is committee-fodder, it doesn't matter how dull they are, I do see that," said Uncle Peter. "I'll have the marmalade please Bill, when you've quite finished slopping it down the outside of the jar."

"Sorry. I can't make the spoon balance across the top. You have a go," Bill slid the marmalade towards Uncle Peter.

"Were you wearing the right thing?" Rachel asked her mother.

"Absolutely, but anything would have done."

"Women!" said Uncle Peter, battling unsuccessfully with the sticky marmalade spoon. "Thank God I wasn't born one. 'The right thing'. What a fuss!"

"Nonsense! There's really only one rule nowadays and that's not to hurt people's feelings," said Aunt Gwen. "And not to make yourself look ridiculous. It's all very well for the young, but——"

"Here we go again," muttered Patrick. "The generation gap——"

"But it's the young who like to *make* the difference," Aunt Gwen retorted. "Who's always saying, 'you can't do that at your age'?"

"You, mostly," said Bill.

"Now come *on*——" Uncle Peter could not resist coming out from behind his paper to join in.

Lucy sat amazed as she always did during such family arguments. To her it had always seemed that grown-ups were grown-ups, and children were children. The grown-ups, were at least thought of, if not referred to, as 'elders and betters', and they'd been treated as such. She had never dreamed that grown-ups and children could join in friendly, and sometimes frankly stupid arguments as they did in this family. The children showed their parents absolutely no respect, and the parents didn't even seem to mind. It made them seem almost not like grown-ups at all. Just ordinary people.

When the post arrived Lucy hung about hopefully in case there was a letter for her. "I'll write soon," Mr. Thomas had said. How soon was 'soon'? Not that morning, anyhow. Lucy turned sadly away from the others opening Christmas cards. Mr. Thomas was always so busy, and though he'd know she'd want news from home at once, he probably hadn't had a minute to send any. That would be it.

Her cousins set off directly after breakfast to invite the remaining guests, but once again Lucy made an excuse not to go. "It's Mr. Thomas you see, who used to live next door to us. Now that I've written to

Mrs. Belling our other neighbour—I think I ought——"

They shrugged, probably secretly relieved not to have to bother with her, Lucy decided, and blamed feelings of extra unhappiness on them. But deep within herself she knew it had something to do with telling yet another lie. She hadn't even written to Mrs. Belling, and had no intention of writing to Mr. Thomas today. Though he might have written to *her*, she decided fretfully. He'd promised he would, yet post after post brought nothing for her at all.

As soon as the cousins had banged out of the house, Lucy raced upstairs. Unfortunately too fast. For as she rounded a corner at top speed she collided with Aunt Gwen carrying a toppling tower of nylon sheets. Aunt Gwen swayed, Lucy fell, and sheets flopped in all directions.

"Oh dear! How mad! It was all my fault! Are you all right, Lucy? Not hurt? Good." Lucy was picking up the sheets. "I suddenly remembered I couldn't think when I'd last put any clean sheets on the beds. You wouldn't like to give me a hand, would you?"

Of course after that she had to. It was quite fun though, going from room to room with Aunt Gwen who whisked about with tremendous speed and energy. No wonder she got so much *done*.

While she worked she talked in her cheerful, disconnected way. Of the hectic time they'd had moving. ("I kept forgetting things, or putting them away so carefully I haven't found them yet!") Of the school where Rachel and Patrick were. ("I don't know if they do any *work*, but they seem to enjoy themselves very much.") Of the early days of her marriage about which she laughed a good deal. ("It

69

was rather awful—we were as poor as churchmice, and I couldn't cook—still can't, for that matter!—poor old Pete had to put up with a lot!")

Lucy was surprised to hear her aunt talk about being poor. How much money you had, or didn't have, was something Aunt Olive had said nicely-brought-up people never discussed. All the same she found this one-sided kind of conversation easier than most. Even when it began to form into questions ("Did you find what you wanted in the costume books? Are you much of a reader?") she found she could say a little more than just 'yes' or 'no' in answer. There was something about Aunt Gwen that was—well, *encouraging*. Perhaps it was because of this that she suddenly found herself able to ask a question. It was after the beds were finished and they were folding up the discarded sheets that Lucy had breath to ask suddenly, "Aunt Gwen, do you believe in ghosts?"

"Ghosts?" Aunt Gwen stood quite still, a sheet drooping from her fingers so that she looked rather like a ghost herself. "Whatever put them into your head?"

"Nothing. They just seemed to be there."

Aunt Gwen went on with her folding. "I should get them out again, if I were you. Ghosts can be uncomfortable things." She made them sound as ordinary as lumps in a chair, or tight shoes.

"How do you know?" Lucy asked. "Have you seen one?"

Aunt Gwen gave her a very straight look. "No, and I don't intend to. Why, do you think you have?"

This was so unexpectedly near the truth that Lucy was thrown off balance. "No—at least, no—I haven't."

"You don't seem very sure."

70

"Oh yes I am. Quite sure."

Aunt Gwen put a hand on her shoulder. "It's very difficult to be certain about these things, you know. Imagination plays such a large part. But even if you did see, or *think* you saw, anything ghostly you wouldn't be afraid, would you?"

"No I wouldn't." That was honest, anyhow. There was nothing frightening about Alice.

"Good." Aunt Gwen was piling the sheets. "We'll take these downstairs and put them in the machine. Can you carry those? Thank you. Let me know next time you see her, will you?"

"I might," said Lucy. And instantly realised she had fallen into a trap. Artful Aunt Gwen, was Lucy's first thought. Making her give herself away like that. A moment later she was full of wonder which turned to panic. How could she possibly have *known*? Had she too—in spite of what she said—seen Alice? Lucy looked narrowly at her aunt but she seemed quite unconcerned, almost as if she had forgotten what they were talking about. She hadn't, though, because half way down the stairs she said over her shoulders. "There's a prayer the country folk in Cornwall were supposed to have used for years. Do you know it? 'From ghoulies and ghosties and long leggedy beasties and things that go bump in the night, the good Lord deliver us'."

"Yes," said Lucy politely.

Aunt Gwen laughed. "Just in case you ever feel the need of it."

Lucy laughed too, to show she knew this was a joke. But she didn't feel like laughing. It was time for serious thinking. Although Aunt Gwen was beginning to rummage for bowls and mislaid knives, which meant she was going to do some cooking, Lucy was determined not to help her. While the others

71

were out was too good an opportunity to be missed. "It's Mr. Thomas's turn to be written to today," she said firmly. "I'd like to do it now, please."

"Of course, Lucy, if you'd like to," said Aunt Gwen, smiling, and Lucy escaped easily. Too easily. Inside she felt horrible. There was Aunt Gwen trusting her and here she was telling yet another lie to get her own way. It seemed to be becoming a habit. What was the matter with her? She never used to be like this.

She had a moment of fear before she pushed open the creaking attic door. But she need not have worried. Everything was as it was when she had first seen the room. She walked in, closing the door carefully behind her. Now that the time had come, Lucy was not quite sure that she was ready to do . . . what she had planned to do. She sank on to a trunk. 'I've got to think this out,' she told herself, as if she had not been thinking out her problem for hours already.

She shivered slightly as she tried to collect her arguments. She had given up the idea that she had dreamed or imagined Alice. She was far too real. Very well then. She, Lucy, must—somehow—have got into the past. The past of about a hundred years ago, if the books were right.

But how and why had it happened? There must be a key to the mystery somewhere. She thought of stories she knew about time travel. An amulet, a magic carpet, an old doorway—a space machine. There was always *something*. . . . Could be as simple a thing as a mirror? A mirror that was *magic*? It seemed crazy, and yet what else could it have been? Of one thing she was uncomfortably certain: there was a sure way to find out.

'Come on, Lucy, you've *got* to do it!' She stood up unwillingly. The mirror seemed to be waiting for her. Slowly, she threaded her way between the trunks towards it. It was very quiet in the attic. Almost as if it was holding its breath. . .

And then, from far below in the kitchen came the faint but distinct whirr of the washing-machine, doubtless dealing with the sheets. Beside it Aunt Gwen would now be struggling alone with the lunch. Lucy tried to forget this, but it was difficult. She felt too much of a beast, and the sound of the machine would not be ignored. Lucy paused.

"Don't listen," a whispering voice advised her— from inside her own head, presumably. With an effort she obeyed it, moving purposefully towards the mirror. After all, it was now or never. The others would come back any minute, and she might never get another chance. . . .

She reached the stack of frames, the foremost of which held glass. She shivered again. Then she knelt carefully on the floor, bent . . . leant forward . . . closed her eyes for a moment . . . then flicked them open to stare into the mirror.

Its mottled surface showed only her own pale, wide-eyed face. She kept perfectly still, listening intently, but there was nothing to hear except the washing-machine. (Poor, kind Aunt Gwen.) No shrill voice greeted her. No second face appeared in the glass beside her own. She searched the reflection and saw only the corner of a dusty dresser, and part of Pegasus—Dobbin?—No, Pegasus, with flaked paintwork and no mane. Now she dared to turn her head to confirm that she was still in an attic used as a boxroom. No narrow bed. No white-painted furniture. *Nobody.*

Lucy sighed gently, hardly knowing whether to be relieved or disappointed. She got to her feet, rubbing her knees—the floorboards were hard—and frowning. The mirror was *not* the key, then. But if not the mirror—what?

There was no evading a shopping expedition in the afternoon.

"We always go to the same place for our presents," Rachel told her as they got ready. "It's a tiny little street, very old and narrow and full of junk shops. It looks just like an old-fashioned picture. You'll love it."

Junk shops did not sound very loveable to Lucy, but she noticed it was being presumed, as usual, that she'd do what the others did. In defence she said, "I shall wear my best coat this time, whatever you say." Just in case they thought she was going to go trailing round any shops looking like they did.

Rachel did not reply. But when Lucy went downstairs in her new outfit, nothing was said. The others, though clean, were as casually dressed as before. They might have been just—well, anybody.

The bus dropped them in the High Street, but after only a few minutes walking, Patrick led the party into a dark alley-way. Overflowing dustbins stood down one side of it. A thin cat shot from behind one of them. There was a most unpleasant smell. Lucy wrinkled her nose, and held her coat close to her. Bill muttered something to Patrick, who answered with only a few words.

"Well," Lucy clearly heard Bill's aggrieved words. "She doesn't have to be so jolly *grand* about everything!"

Lucy made a face to herself. Surely it wasn't grand not to like dark passages and dirty smells? Any properly brought up person would know that. Alice, for instance. Lucy wished heartily that Alice were with them now. She was tiresome in some ways but

Lucy knew instinctively that in many others they thought alike. 'I could make a real friend of Alice,' she thought wistfully.

A burst of daylight met them as they emerged from the alley under a rounded stone arch.

"There!" said Rachel. "Didn't I say it was just like a picture?"

It certainly was. A narrow lane ran steeply down the side of a hill. On each side of it, only a few feet from each other, were old-fashioned shops with gabled windows and low doors and bow windows.

"It must have looked much the same for centuries," Patrick remarked. "Can't think why they haven't pulled it down to make offices," he added sarcastically.

And if they had, your father would probably have built them, thought Lucy with bitterness.

"Now we'll separate," said Rachel. "Christmas presents *must* be secret or half the fun's gone. Not you, Lucy, of course, because you don't know your way around. You and I'll stick together."

Lucy was secretly grateful for this offer. She had no wish to be abandoned in this strange district, nor to struggle with Christmas presents for almost-unknown relations. But even as she was about to say, "Thank you, I'd like that," a perverse thought came into her head. Was Rachel being genuinely kind, or did she merely think Lucy was too young and stupid to be left alone to shop? Almost against her will she said, "There's no need to worry about *me*. I can manage."

"Are you sure?" Rachel looked taken aback. "I mean—you don't know your way around here. What about getting home?"

"If Bill can manage I suppose I can," Lucy said in a haughty voice most unlike her own.

"Yes, but he's done it before, and——Never mind, It's a twenty-two bus to the end of our road."

"Thank you," said Lucy.

Rachel looked at her doubtfully for a few seconds, then shrugged. "O.K. If that's how you want it, I'll be on my way."

Lucy watched her go. Rachel was glad of a chance to abandon her. They all were, she told herself. Very well. She could do without them. Easily. She had almost forgotten that it was she herself who had insisted on being left.

It was funny to be shopping alone, in a place she didn't know. She looked carefully down the little cobbled street. One crooked window was full of musical instruments. The next glinted with old silver. A very muddly window of second-hand clothes all looking rather dirty came next, and then another antique shop. She put her hot forehead against the cold glass of the window. Inside lay trays of old rings, brooches and pendants. One of these reminded her of one which Aunt Olive used to wear. A rush of the old homesickness came over her. Next to the jewelry was displayed a collection of old glass paperweights. Behind them stood a row of copper vessels: sauce-pans, narrow-necked jugs, a large round cauldron. Lucy, gazing idly at its rounded surface smiled as she saw how its curve made her face look pear-shaped. Another shopper paused behind her. The cauldron showed another pear-shaped face—a much whiskered one under a top hat. . . . A *top* hat?

Lucy turned curiously to see it better and was in time to see the owner's long hooded overcoat disappear in the crowd. And *what* a crowd! She stared. And stared again. Women with bustled coats to their button-boots, and little bonnets like decorated pan-cakes. Two little girls, similarly dressed, a terribly ragged little boy with huge eyes in a white face, bare feet. Many top-hats, often raised at the sight of a lady.

Lucy blinked. She put a hand behind her to steady herself against the frame of the shop-window, for an increasing sensation of unreality made her sway a little, and the pins and needles were back. Her eyes took in odd details: a furry muff on a ribbon; a little boy carrying a hoop; a fashionable haberdasher's had replaced the old-clothes shop, and where the silver shop had been, there was a bakery. . . .

"I've done it again," she told herself. "I've gone back. But I don't understand——"

Indeed she could hardly think at all for the muzziness in her head. Perhaps it was partly the noise that made her feel so stupid—for there was a tremendous mixture of sounds all round her. A dirty old woman with a tattered shawl and long greasy curls was screeching at people to buy her trinkets. Rough little boys shouted as they dodged through the shoppers. From somewhere close came tinkling music, and in the distance a cry of 'Milk—o! Milk—o!'

A small figure came hurrying through the others. "Ah, there you are!" cried Alice. Her quick gaze flicked up and down Lucy. She bent closer to whisper. "I like your new coat. Much more suitable, though you really ought to wear a hat and gloves outdoors, you know. It's vulgar not to. Never mind, your taste is improving."

"Now look here!" began Lucy indignantly. "I've had this coat for——" And then, as before, came the feeling that after all what did it matter if Alice believed her or not? Alice was so wrong about so many things that one more didn't matter. "How did you know I'd be here?" she asked instead.

77

Alice put on her sly look. "That would be telling, wouldn't it?"

"Yes it would," retorted Lucy. "And I want to know."

"Then want must be your master," said Alice. "Now don't get cross again. Mademoiselle will be here at any minute—I had to trick her to get away. When she comes, don't say anything. I'll explain you."

"But I don't want to be explained."

"Oh yes you do," said Alice. "You can't explain yourself, can you?"

Lucy knew this to be true, though at that moment she could not quite have said why. In any case there was no time to try for a tall faded woman, dressed in black, was hurrying towards them. "The little Aleece! You bad girl! Méchante! Méchante petite fille! What 'ave you been doing?"

"I saw Lucy, the friend that I told you about," said Alice. "She was all by herself, and I knew you wouldn't want me to leave her alone."

"All by herself?" Mademoiselle looked anxiously at Lucy. "Why is theese?" Her parchment-coloured face was lined with concern.

"She has no one to look after her," said Alice. "Her Mama and Papa are away, just like mine, only she hasn't got a nice governess to look after her like I have." She smiled winningly at Mademoiselle, who looked scandalised.

"But a nursemaid? Somebody? Oui?"

"Oh yes, there is a nursemaid," said Alice. "But she is too busy looking after Lucy's four little brothers and sisters. She's quite cruel to Lucy."

"But, no!"

"No," Lucy agreed, horrified to hear so many lies.

"Now Lucy, it's much better that Mademoiselle should *know*," said Alice, pinching Lucy's arm. "Isn't it dreadful, Mademoiselle?" She went on rapidly. "Today the nursemaid said, 'Go for a walk by yourself and don't come back until tea-time'!"

Mademoiselle threw up her hands. "Tea-time? *Impossible!*"

"Oh yes, impossible," said Alice. "So she must come home to dinner with us, and she can, can't she? Do say yes!"

"I do not know what to say," said Mademoiselle helplessly. "Her Mama—"

"Her Mama is a great friend of my Mama's," said Alice, "and I know Mama would like Lucy to come and play with me whenever she can."

"But yes," said Mademoiselle. "That would be better. You should not be on the streets alone, my child."

She looked so kindly at Lucy that she was ashamed to let the governess go on believing this preposterous tale but before she could say anything, Mademoiselle cried "Allons!" and began to lead the way home.

"But—" Lucy began. There was something else she should be doing, she was sure, and somewhere else that she should be, though strangely she could not remember exactly what these things were. Alice took her hand in a hard grip. "Don't say anything!" she warned, "or I'll pinch you again, much harder."

It was not fear of being pinched again which kept Lucy silent on the way home, but wonder at everything she saw and heard.

"Oh look!" she cried, when they came to the source of the music—a barrel organ with a tiny monkey in a red jacket capering on a chain beside it.

"Punch and Judy!" she exclaimed a few minutes

79

later as they came across a tall striped booth around which a crowd of grubby children was gathered.

But neither Mademoiselle nor Alice were interested in these things. "Come along, or we'll never get there!" Alice urged her, while Mademoiselle steered them anxiously past beggars and over muddy cobbles. Horses clip-clopped noisily by, drawing a variety of carts and carriages, even an open-topped bus. Part of Lucy knew to expect these sights; another, more buried part, was amazed and fascinated. She was so busy staring round her that she was quite surprised to find they were in the familiar square. There were smart new houses round it, though the same pool was in the middle. Now they were in the carriage-way and Mademoiselle was pulling at the front door bell. The door was opened by a girl in cap and apron.

"Flo," Alice hissed, and Lucy was able to wonder fleetingly what the girl would say if she knew the visitor had already been trespassing in her bedroom.

There was hardly time to look at the hall before they were upstairs. "What are you wearing under your coat?" Alice whispered.

Lucy held it open to reveal a tiny pleated skirt and a matching jersey knitted by Aunt Olive.

"Oh!" exclaimed Alice in disgust. "Look at your *legs showing*! Don't let Mademoiselle see. She would be *so* shocked! Come to my bedroom and we'll find a frock of mine for you. You're smaller than me, but there are *hundreds* that I've outgrown!"

Lucy was happy to follow Alice into her bedroom. (But hadn't she herself slept here once with somebody else?) A big mahogany wardrobe held a row of lovely clothes: coats and capes and mantles and dresses all in the most beautiful stuffs. Lucy fingered them lovingly. Frills and tucks and pleats abounded.

The materials of the party dresses felt wonderfully grand; velvets, taffetas, silks, organdies.

Alice saw her gazing enviously. "Try them on if you like. All of them. I don't mind."

"May I really?"

But when Lucy took off her jersey and skirt Alice was horrified. "Oh you poor thing! You're hardly wearing anything! Haven't you got any proper drawers? Or combinations? And your petticoat!" She took Lucy's nylon slip between her fingers. "What can it be made of? Oh poor, poor Lucy!"

"I'm not poor, I'm an heiress," said Lucy struggling into a white party dress.

"Don't tell stories!" said Alice tartly. "That dress needs a sash." Alice pulled out a drawer. "Look, here's a pink one, here's a blue one. Which will you try?"

Lucy tried them both and then almost everything else in the cupboard. How Aunt Olive would have loved these beautiful clothes!

An hour raced by. Alice enjoyed herself as much as Lucy did. "There! See how nice you look in that white dress! I know!" Alice actually clapped her hands, "You shall wear it! For my birthday party. Mama has said I may have one, and of course you must be there! Look, this is the new one I'm going to wear!" She showed Lucy a white dress sprigged with rosebuds. "Oh, it does seem a shame you can't have proper clothes! Would you let Papa adopt you?"

"Of course I wouldn't!"

"I think he might, if I persuaded him. Do say I may try," Alice wheedled. "I would so like you to come and live here with me."

"Don't be stupid, you know I can't," said Lucy.

She was vague about why exactly this was so, but certain of it.

"There's no such word as can't," Alice retorted at once. "If you don't say you'll come I'll—I'll—make you."

"You couldn't," said Lucy doubtfully.

"Oh couldn't I? Don't start being disagreeable again, because you don't know what I can do."

This was uncomfortably true. Lucy frowned. "Alice," she said slowly, "when I'm not here, how do you know where to find me?"

"You're always here," said Alice. "At last. I've waited and waited so long. . ."

"How long?" Lucy asked quickly.

"Too long," said Alice. "That's why now you've come, I wish you'd stay."

"But I can't be in two places at once," Lucy protested.

"No," said Alice. Her expression became thoughtful, then cunning. "No, you can't be in two places at once, can you?"

And there was something about the way she said it which touched Lucy with fear.

Chapter Six

"So you'd much better stay with me," Alice went on "and be my very own friend. It's so lonely having only Mademoiselle. Mama and Papa have been abroad a long time you know. They *say* they're going to find a house in the country so that we can all live together again. But I don't know when that will be. . . So you mustn't leave me till then."

"I shall," said Lucy uneasily. "In fact I'm going back now." She climbed swiftly out of the gingham dress Alice had lent her.

"You can't," said Alice, quickly.

"Oh can't I?" said Lucy, already in her jersey. But her nervous fingers fumbled with the zip of her skirt. (For how indeed could she get back?) She reached for her coat.

"I shan't let you," said Alice, "and if you try, I'll make something awful happen to you!"

She looked so fierce that Lucy almost believed the threat. Again she was chilled with fear. But why, she asked herself, should I be afraid of Alice? She's only another little girl after all. (But was she?) A phrase seemed to float towards her out of the air. "From ghoulies and ghosties. . ." she murmured.

"What?" cried Alice.

83

"And long-legged beasties. . ." The words were absurd, but they brought with them the picture of a kind laughing face. She glanced automatically into the glass to make sure her collar was straight.

"Stop that!" said Alice sharply, darting between Lucy and the mirror, her face twisted with anger. But she was too late. The reflections of a brass bed strewn with clothes which had framed their figures had already dissolved. Lucy covered her eyes. When she removed her hand it was to see instead the modern bedroom with which she was familiar. Dizziness made her sway. She sat down suddenly on the nearest bed.

"Oh——" she moaned faintly.

Rachel burst in, her arms full of parcels.

"What on earth's the matter with you?" she asked.

*   *   *

"She says she wasn't feeling sick or anything, but honestly, Mum, she did look awful. Sort of yellow and staring."

"And then what happened?"

"Nothing, really. I said should I fetch you and she said no, so I hung about a bit and she gradually began to look a bit more ordinary and then . . . that was all."

"Has she seemed ill to you before?"

Rachel thought. "Not ill. But quite often sort of not-there, if you know what I mean."

Aunt Gwen sighed. "Too well. I think she must have taken the death of that aunt very hard. Does she ever talk about her?"

"Never. But then we don't start it. You said not to."

"I wonder if I was wrong. She seems so withdrawn. Look, darling, thank you for telling me. I

84

think I'll have a word with Dad. Perhaps we'll ask Dr. Brown to have a look at her. She might need a tonic or something."

"It'll take more than a tonic to put her right," said Rachel.

* * *

Dr. Brown was tall, oldish, and had quite a quiet way of speaking which reminded Lucy of Mr. Thomas. In the ordinary way she could have been prepared to like him, but now she was full of suspicion. Why had he been sent for? What was supposed to be wrong with her? Aunt Gwen, when asked, had said cheerfully, "Everybody needs a check up now and again," but Lucy had not been satisfied.

After he had examined her carefully he said, "There doesn't seem to be much wrong with this young lady," and began to put his instruments back in his bag. Aunt Gwen murmured something about notes for a meeting and slipped from the room. Lucy was left alone with the doctor. Now was her chance.

"What I don't understand is what was supposed to be wrong with me."

Dr. Brown perched himself on the edge of a chair. "When people can't eat, and start talking in their sleep, it usually means they're not feeling absolutely a hundred percent."

"I eat all right," Lucy said defensively. "And I didn't know about sleep talking."

"Rachel does, you ask her."

"She might have told me."

"Any idea what you might have been talking about?"

"No."

"Your Aunt Olive perhaps?" So he knew all about her.

"No."

"Anything else on your mind?"

Lucy hesitated. "Not really."

"You can say anything to doctors, you know. They're never surprised, and never shocked."

She looked at Dr. Brown's kind lined face, and thought: 'Suppose I told him that I was getting to know a ghost? He'd be surprised then all right. *And* shocked.' She said nothing.

"Get on with your cousins all right?" asked Dr. Brown.

"Yes thank you," said Lucy automatically in her polite voice.

He put his head on one side. "You don't have to say that, you know. Making friends can be a slow and difficult business, and you've only been here a week."

A week! Was it as long as that?

"And if you're not getting a proper night's sleep then days seem difficult to get through, don't they? What do you think about before you go to sleep?"

Alice. For the last three nights she had thought of scarcely anything else. Alice's anger. Alice crying, 'I'll make something awful happen to you!' Lucy looked up into the doctor's kind face. "Nothing special."

"You can tell me the truth."

She hung her head. She couldn't tell the truth now to him or to anyone else. It was too strange, too frightening. They'd never believe her. And Alice would be furious. She shuddered.

"Once when I was a boy," said Dr. Brown, "I saw a house on fire in the middle of the night. It was miles from my own home, where there was no danger of fire at all, but I couldn't get it out of my mind: its orange glow in the sky, the leaping flames, the terror lest somebody had been burnt. I thought about it all the time. It was bad enough by day, but after I was in bed at night it was quite unbearable. And the most dreadful thing of all was that I couldn't tell anyone." He paused. Lucy watched him intently. "The longer I kept my fear to myself the worse it became. I talked in my sleep too, and when I did sleep I had the most terrible nightmares. I became quite ill with worry.

"One day I simply couldn't bear it any longer. I told my father everything. At first I was afraid he'd laugh, but he didn't. He went all around the house showing me the fire escapes, and the other safety measures. But best of all he just listened while I talked. And that was what cured my unreasonable terror of fire."

Lucy knew the story had been told to comfort her, but she thought it might very well likely be true. "It must have been lovely. Like a spell being broken."

"Just like that. And such a simple method too. It works for all the fears people have, like fear of growing up, or not being able to do lessons, or a new baby becoming too important, or the dark, or having to leave home or someone you love, or getting shut up in a room, or of death itself. Dozens of things."

"And they can all be cured just by talking about them?"

"It always helps enormously."

For a moment Lucy was tempted to tell him everything, however unbelievable it sounded. Then she remembered there was more than one way of being ill. If Dr. Brown decided she had a disordered mind he might send her for hospital treatment and that she did not want. Besides, Alice fitted nowhere into the lists of fears he had mentioned. She pressed her lips together.

Dr. Brown stood up, shook hands, and said goodbye. He smiled as he spoke but Lucy knew he was disappointed that she hadn't confided in him.

Aunt Gwen now became more harassed than ever. Like the Tuesday party, Christmas seemed to come as a surprise to her. "What? Less than a fortnight from today? You're joking!"

"Only if they've changed the date this year," Uncle Peter said drily. "In my experience it's usually celebrated on December 25th."

Aunt Gwen flipped wildly through her diary. "You're right. Oh my goodness! Why didn't somebody *tell* me?"

"We had been sort of hinting for some time," Rachel said.

"And there are lots of little clues if you're observant enough to look for them," Patrick said. "Things like us being home for the Christmas holidays, and the shops full of decorations, and that we've been getting Christmas cards all this week."

"I know we have, but I thought they were just well-organised people posting early."

"No," Bill told her. "Just other *dis*organised people posting late."

Aunt Gwen groaned. "You'll have to help me, all of you. I haven't done a thing! I don't know where to begin!"

"Always begin at the beginning, go on to the end, and then stop," suggested Uncle Peter helpfully.

"Pete! How can you just sit there doing nothing?"

"I'm sitting here doing nothing because presently I intend to do a great deal of hard work which I had already planned, having a suspicion the festive season might sneak up on you yet again. This afternoon I'm going into town to get a tree, and some decorations."

"Mum, would you like me to rush out and buy a million cards?" Rachel offered.

"If you'd be an angel. Do try to steer clear of the glittery ones with terrible words inside."

"We send you merry Christmas cheer," Patrick began to chant, "with all our wishes most sincere, for all you wish yourself this year——"

"Shut up," said Rachel briefly. "It's bad enough getting that kind without you making them up."

Patrick refused to be quenched. "There should be an annual competition for the most awful."

"St. Valentine's day would be even better," Bill suggested. "This is the time for fondest greeting, lots of little lovebirds meeting——"

"Meeting!" Aunt Gwen clasped her head. "I should be at one this very minute!"

"Well you're not," said Uncle Peter. "Give it a miss. They can get on very well without you."

"What, when I'm Secretary?" Aunt Gwen rushed from the room, and from the indulgent laughter of everyone else.

"So much for Christmas as far as your mother's concerned," said Uncle Peter. "But I expect the rest of us can sort it out between us."

"Bill and I'll give you a hand getting the decorations up," Patrick promised. "We're dab hands at that."

"Thanks. That's fine then. Everybody's-——no, Lucy! What's your strong line?"

Lucy flushed. As usual in this household she felt she hadn't got a strong line. Then she had an idea. "Cooking?" she suggested tentatively.

They fell on her. "You can cook?"

She had been unprepared for quite so much incredulous enthusiasm. "Er—a little," she admitted cautiously.

"That's fixed then," said Patrick. "Chief cook and bottle washer. Why didn't you tell us before?"

"You didn't ask," said Lucy simply.

"We are asking now and in a big way," said Uncle Peter. "So be warned. What can you do?"

In her mind, Lucy ran over Aunt Olive's painstaking lessons in the kitchen. Nothing ambitious or fancy had been involved as they could not have afforded it. But she realised now with a rush of gratitude how useful the lessons had indeed turned out to be. "Christmas cake?" she hazarded.

"Done!" said Bill.

"I suppose," said Patrick "you wouldn't know anything about mince pies?"

Mince pies had been one of Aunt Olive's specialities. She had always given Mr. Thomas a dozen at Christmas. Lucy thought now of the carefully packed box with sheets of foil between every layer, the whole finished with a ribbon. Who would do them for him this year? Her eyes pricked, but she was able to say, "I think I can do them, more or less," and was again an immediate success. She must buy all the ingredients they told her. Uncle Peter would give her the money. She could start a lovely cook-in that very afternoon.

Lucy was half afraid Aunt Gwen might be offended when she heard of this plan but she was delighted. "My dearest child! You can cook? What a merciful providence! Nobody else can. Yes, of course you can have the kitchen to yourself. I shall be out anyway."

So Lucy spent the afternoon measuring and mixing, and rolling pastry. The rest of the family was warned sternly to keep out of her way which made her feel pleasantly important. There was a great deal of washing-up to do at the end but she didn't mind.

Three dozen mince pies already in the oven and the cake was waiting its turn. Perhaps tomorrow she would offer to make a macaroni cheese for supper.

Someone turned on the radio full blast in the sitting room. It was a choir singing 'Silent Night'.

"Oh listen," shrilled Rachel's loud voice. "My absolutely favourite carol!"

It made Christmas seem closer than ever. She remembered that while she had been cooking Uncle Peter and the boys had been putting up the decorations. She could almost smell the strong sweet piney scent of the tree. She imagined it lit with rainbow coloured lights and hung with the kind of tiny trinkets Aunt Olive had saved so carefully from long ago. She could see the outlines of the house as they would be softened by clusters of holly. So much more like a home. She felt warm and relaxed.

And she realised that she had not once during the afternoon even thought of Alice.

But when she finally emerged flushed and triumphant from the kitchen the sight that met her eyes was a terrible shock. Everything seemed to have turned blue: ice blue glittering streamers looped across the hall. There were more in the sitting room. Clusters of blue and silver glass bells hung over each doorway. And a blue tinsel kissing-ring hung over the stairs. And the tree! Instead of the lovely dark green fragrant thing Lucy had expected there stood an imitation one. Blue of course. Only witch balls were hung on it, blue and silver. They were glittered into life by hundreds of tiny white lights. No colour anywhere, no warmth.

"How do you like it, Lucy?" Uncle Peter stood back, a hammer in his hand to admire the effect.

She couldn't say anything. She thought it was too

dreadful for words. All the lovely old-fashionedness of Christmas replaced by this sham cold tinsel.

Aunt Gwen answered for her. "It's fantastic, Pete! It really is."

Yes, it really was. Fantastic was the word. Like some terrible nightmare.

"The best we've had yet, I think," Patrick was saying with satisfaction.

"It should be," Bill licked his thumb tenderly. "It's caused more injuries than any other year."

"Well, that's my lot," said Uncle Peter. "You boys can put the steps and tools away and Rachel clear up the debris. I'm for a cup of coffee." He went into the den with Aunt Gwen.

Rachel began to scoop up short lengths of silver ribbon and tinsel. "You haven't said anything yet, Lucy."

"No. It's so—so different."

"Isn't it?" Rachel said with satisfaction. "We have a new theme each year. Once it was all cotton wool snowmen and robins, too old-fashioned for anything. Last year it was scarlet and gold but it was rather like living inside a Christmas cracker. This is the best yet, don't you think? So frosty."

"A bit cold-looking?" Lucy suggested carefully.

"You don't like it do you? Be honest."

She searched for words that would say what she meant without sounding hurtful. Before she could find them she heard a voice—could it really be her own?—say: "I think it's perfectly hateful!"

"I say—" began Bill indignantly.

"There's no need to be *that* honest," said Patrick.

"Rachel said I was to be," Lucy said weakly. But although she was truly appalled by what she had said, she found that now she had begun she could not stop herself going on in the same unkind way.

92

"Christmas *should* be old-fashioned. That's what it's all about. It ought to be—well, *warm* and—and—pretty. This," she glanced scornfully round the blue glittering room, "looks exactly like a *shop!* It's vulgar!"

There was a heavy silence in which the cousins looked at each other. Then Patrick spoke. "The trouble is, Lucy, that you don't like us or anything about us, do you?"

She faced the three of them. "I didn't say that."

"You don't have to. You've made it pretty clear since you first came here. Everything we do or say is wrong by your standards."

"Patrick, I don't think——"

"Don't butt in, Rachel. It's better to get it out in the open. Lucy, we have tried. What is it that you can't take?"

Anger and disappointment over what she considered the spoiling of Christmas, and a wave of grief for Aunt Olive and all she stood for gave Lucy a courage she didn't know she had. "You're all peculiar. You don't even know how odd you are! It's because you seem to think that everything's got to be new, different, changed. This was a perfectly nice old house before your father started ruining it with his built-in cupboards and modern ideas. And you're just the same. Look at the way you dress! And don't even have proper meals. Most people are having tea at this time but not you. You have meals just when you think you will. That's because even your mother has to be different, tearing about to meetings instead of looking after you and letting you go out alone and even forgetting Christmas—*forgetting Christmas!* She's so——"

Patrick cut in, sharply. "That's enough about Mum, thank you. But you might care to know that though she may forget some of the trimmings like cards and food and decorations, she doesn't forget what it's really all about. It's a time for being *kind*, you know. Considerate. Dull things like that. Not for being rude and hurtful and——"

Bill's face was scarlet with anger as he broke in. "I suppose you've never thought it might be you that's different? Just because you've been shut up all those years with that crazy old aunt——"

Lucy's hand shot out. Bill leapt away only just in time, as Rachel grabbed at her wrist.

"Let go!" shrieked Lucy, breaking away.

She put her hands over her ears. Her voice sounded odd inside her own head. "I won't listen! I don't want to hear another word! I want to be quiet, *quiet* for once—as if you even know what quietness *means!*"

She turned and raced upstairs, slammed the door behind her and flung herself face downwards on her bed. How cruel, heartless, beastly! They didn't care anything for her or her troubles. They went on doing everything their own way expecting her to join in and when she didn't they blamed her. She remembered Bill's words, 'shut up with a crazy old aunt'. How *dared* they, how *dared* they, when they'd never met dear kind gentle Aunt Olive! She ground her face into the pillow but she was too angry to cry.

*   *   *

The snow began during supper. Bill saw it first and called excitedly to the others. Together they watched the flakes fluttering in the light of the street lamp.

"Not the kind to lie though," Rachel said regretfully. "Too small and spitty. It'll turn to rain in a minute." But all the same they could not resist peering from between the curtains every now and then to make sure it hadn't. Lucy sighed deeply as she watched the swirling flakes. Two years ago Aunt Olive had let her go tobogganning with the Belling children. Finding them rough and noisy she had been glad when it was time to go home, but now she would happily have been back with them in a district she knew amongst people who cared about her.

"But *I* care about you!"

Lucy jumped, startled to hear the words spoken so close to her ear. Who had said them?

Uncle Peter was frowning over a plan, his three children absorbed at the next window. She must have been imagining things. And yet the words had been so clear. . . .

"Listen!" said Bill. "Can you hear what I hear?"

"Mum throwing things about in the kitchen you mean?" queried Patrick.

"No, stupid. Listen!"

Even Uncle Peter looked up at the urgency in his voice. And then—quite clearly—they all heard them: carol singers.

"God rest you merry gentlemen,
 Let nothing you dismay."

The words became louder as the group approached the gate. And paused huddled under their lanterns to sing.

"Oh look! They're in fancy dress!" cried Rachel. "Dad, do look! Get Mum, somebody!"

"All giving orders and no *do*—just like a girl!" grumbled Patrick, but he darted off to fetch Aunt Gwen. When she saw the tableau at the gate she was as excited as any of them. "What a wonderful sight! I didn't know people bothered to do that kind of thing nowadays. Peter, do go and ask them in."

"They'll be on a highly organised tour, collecting

for some charity I expect," said Uncle Peter, but he went to the study to fetch some money.

"Tidings of comfort and joy, comfort and joy!" carolled the choir.

Lucy, watching, suddenly stiffened. Had a figure detached itself from the group and run, crouched, towards the house?

She looked round the family in the room. No one else seemed to have noticed anything. She put her face close to the pane to see better. Yes, a head was bobbing among the bushes by the window.

"I wonder who dressed them?" mused Aunt Gwen. "Their costumes look perfect in every detail from here." She swished the curtain as she spoke in order to see better, and for the peering Lucy the light was suddenly changed so that instead of the dark garden she saw only a reflection of the room behind her and of her own face. Yes, of course it was her own face. It had to be. But even as she reasoned, the owner of the face raised a pale hand that beckoned.

Lucy, with a thrill of fear, shook her head. But the other head nodded. The lights in the room swung, the lights in the reflection swung, wild half-formed ideas swung in Lucy's head. She saw the mouth on the other side of the window frame the words, "Come with me!"

For a moment she hesitated.

Then, unnoticed by anyone else, she slipped from the room and ran out into the snowy night.

Chapter Seven

"Put this cloak on," ordered Alice.

"But I don't see——"

"Never mind what *you* see. Think of what somebody else might see. Hurry up!"

At the well-remembered imperious tone Lucy obediently threw the cloak round her shoulders.

"And put the hood up. That's right. Wasn't it a good idea of mine to bring an extra cloak?" She gave Lucy's arm a squeeze. "I knew you'd come."

"I didn't," Lucy said flatly. "And I wasn't sure it was you in the garden at first."

"Who else would it be?" Alice chuckled. "Especially after that splendid tantrum of yours! I didn't know you could be so vexing!"

Lucy looked at her sideways. "How did you know about that?"

"I can always find out things when I want to. Nearly always, anyway. . . . Look, we are falling behind the others. We must catch up."

"Who are the others?"

"The stout lady is Mrs. Naylor, a friend of Mama's. That is why I am invited. I asked if I could bring a young friend to keep me company."

"But you couldn't know you'd be able to——"

Lucy began to object, but already a strange feeling that she belonged to this party made the question seem irrelevant.

"I said your governess would bring you to meet us," Alice said easily. "And don't ask so many questions. After all, you wanted to come."

"Did I?"

"Of course, or I couldn't have——Now stop arguing, because it's time to sing."

"What are we collecting for?"

"Collecting for?" Alice's lantern-lit face was uncomprehending.

"Surely we are trying to make money?"

" 'Make money?' What a vulgar idea. We're not street urchins!" Alice tossed her head. "Mrs. Naylor runs a choir, and tonight we are calling on a few friends—they know we are coming—to give pleasure."

Lucy thought of the ragged children she had seen in the streets. Surely it would not have been vulgar, but a good thing to collect money for them? But they were all now stopping outside a very grand front door. "The Holly and the Ivy," announced Mrs. Naylor, in a rich voice. She hummed a note. The choir burst into the carol. At the end of it the big front door swung open. A tall butler informed Mrs. Naylor that the lady of the house was awaiting them in the drawing-room.

And *what* a drawing-room! It might have been a page of Aunt Olive's album which had sprung to life. Here were the many little tables, the china cabinet, the ornaments, the wax flowers under glass domes, the grand piano. Most splendid of all was a green, spicy Christmas tree, lit with, yes, real wax candles. (Why did they not set it blazing?) Fragile baubles, glass birds, glittering ornaments swung amongst the green branches. It was all a proper Christmas tree should have been.

The room was thronged by grand ladies and gentlemen. The latter were in clothes rather like those worn by waiters. The ladies wore beautiful bustled gowns, nipped in at the waist and trailing on the ground. Their hair was curled in piles, their shoulders were bare and white. Jewels sparkled in their hair, their ears, round their necks and arms.

Lucy could only gasp with admiration till Alice gave her a sharp nudge. "Keep your cloak wrapped closely round you." So when everyone else removed theirs in the warm room, she shook her head. "She has a slight chill," Alice explained for her.

Lucy was kindly welcomed as 'Alice's little friend.' The butler reappeared with two frilly maids. They carried silver trays loaded with mince-pies, tiny cakes of marzipan, and most delicious of all, crystallised fruits of many kinds. Alice and Lucy were pressed to refresh themselves till they could eat no more. At last, in spite of protests, Mrs. Naylor said the party must leave, as they had promised to visit two other houses that night. So they sang 'Good King Wenceslas' and the house-guests joined in. The big fire crackled, the big tree twinkled, all was glitter and light and friendliness.

It was quite a shock to be once more in the cold street. The gas-lights still lit whirling flakes, but they were smaller. "You were right," Lucy whispered. "It *is* too spitty to lie."

"I'm sure I never said anything so hateful!"

"I distinctly remember——" But did she? Had it been Alice who had made that remark? If not, who? Lucy could not think. And she no longer really cared. It was as if the magic of Christmas had laid its spell on her so that she no longer *wanted to*.

More walking through slush, more singing, another festive drawing-room hospitably ready to receive them. Lucy was yawning long before they reached the last house.

"Never mind," said Alice, seeing this. "You're staying with me tonight."

"No, I'm not." Somehow she was sure of that.

"You are. I've arranged it with Mademoiselle. You can't think how many fibs I had to tell. You must come now."

"I can't. They'll worry if I don't go back."

"There's no one who truly worries about you except me, Lucy. Oh dear, now I see you're going to get cross again. Please don't. You can borrow my best night-dress, and tomorrow morning we will have breakfast together at a little table with a white cloth before the fire. You'd like that. . ."

Yes, she would. All the same, something stirred uneasily at the back of her mind.

"That's settled then," Alice said with satisfaction. "You'll get used to our ways very quickly, and *want* to stay for always."

"No," said Lucy, her unease increasing. "I must go back to the others, or they'll try to find me."

"But they won't know where to look, will they?" Even in the dark she could hear the subtle change in Alice's voice. "You haven't told them about me. Have you?"

"No—no———"

"Then they can't find you! You'll be safe with me."

But safe was suddenly what Lucy didn't feel. Somehow she sensed a trap had been laid for her and that she was on the point of falling into it.

"I'm going now," she said.

Alice clutched her cloak. "You don't know how to."

"I do." But it was another lie. She had no idea. Was there no one here who could help her? She looked hopefully into the faces of the carollers, but they only smiled kindly back at her. Alice also wore a smile, but hers was of a different kind. Sly. Triumphant. Malicious?

Lucy shivered in the moonlight.

*   *   *

"But I didn't see her go," Rachel protested. "We were all looking out of the window, remember? Except Dad who'd gone to get some money. And suddenly she wasn't there."

"I can't understand it." Her mother paced up and down the sitting-room. "Why should she dash out into the night without even taking a coat? The child'll be frozen. Pete, don't you think you ought to ring the police?"

"No need to be that dramatic." But there was something about the way he said it that made the boys look at each other. "After all, she hasn't been gone two hours yet."

"But two hours——in this weather!"

Rachel looked at Patrick in a worried way, and he answered the look. Their father saw them. "Are you two quite sure you don't know more than you're letting on?"

"Not absolutely sure," Patrick admitted. "There was a spot of bother earlier."

"You'd better tell us about it," said his father quietly.

"Well, it began about the decorations. . . ." By the time he had ended the account his father was looking grave. "Why didn't you tell us this before? Don't you see that it might make all the difference?"

"Between what and what?" Bill asked nervously.

"Between Lucy escaping to be by herself—as I gather she has before—and Lucy running away."

"Oh no!" Rachel was horrified. "Not *really* running? Mum, you don't think——?"

"I hardly know what to think, darling. Except that we ought to do something. Now."

"Not the police, please! Not yet."

Her mother put her arms round her. "She's not our child and we're responsible for her."

"What about those people she used to know, Dad?" suggested Patrick. "That clergyman chap, for instance? If Lucy runs anywhere, it might be there."

"That's an idea. Thomas. We could give him a ring. If she isn't with him, he might be able to give us some idea of where she might be making for. And exactly what it is she's running away from. I'm sure we shall find her somewhere safe and sound. But if it turns out that any child—however unusual or difficult—has run away from my house because of unkindness——" He didn't finish.

The cousins looked miserably at each other.

Their father dialled Mr. Thomas's number.

Rachel crept away while the call was being put through. She could bear it no longer. Certainly Lucy had been horrible this afternoon. But miserable too, she was sure of it. There'd been something wretched about her white face as she'd spat out those cutting words in a voice so spiteful that it had hardly sounded like Lucy's quiet one at all. And after that no one had spoken to her more than they could help. So that finally she'd rushed out into the snow rather than stay in the same house with them another moment. Rachel could hardly imagine what it must feel like to be as unhappy as that.

She opened the big front door and huddled in the cold porch, staring into the clearing night.

"Lucy," she said aloud. "Come back. Please come back, wherever you are. We're sorry, and I'm sure you are too." The wind whined round the house, but there was no other answer to her plea. Rachel stared into the dark, willing a small figure to appear out of it. Tears crawled down her cheeks. "Lucy, Lucy!"

*   *   *

The snow had quite stopped. Stars hung overhead. "Our old favourite now," said Mrs. Naylor. At her signal, her choir softly started the first line:

"Silent night! Holy night!"

'Our old favourite' Mrs. Naylor had said. But it was somebody else's favourite too. Whose . . . *whose?* Lucy fought to emerge from the cobwebs round her brain. Some one else had said 'my absolute favourite' . . . *Rachel!* The name came to her from nowhere, but suddenly, strongly.

"Sing!" commanded Alice fiercely at her side.

Rachel who? . . . and where——? But no matter. Rachel who was unhappy. She must get back to her. . . . She was aware that Alice was watching her closely. "See the gentle mother and Child," sang Lucy uncertainly. "Holy—holy——?"

"Concentrate!"

'I am concentrating,' thought Lucy grimly, 'more than you realise.' She struggled to remember exactly who Rachel was. Alice's obvious scrutiny, and her constant interruptions were making thought difficult. The first step, then, was to free herself of Alice.

"Rest in Heavenly peace!" sang Lucy loudly.

Alice gave a little smile, apparently satisfied.

"Silent night! Holy night!" Lucy took a step backwards. Alice seemed not to notice. "Guiding star, lend thy light!" Another step away. "See the Eastern—" *Now!*

But as Lucy tried to run, she was pulled up with a jerk. So Alice had been ready after all! "Aha!" she hissed angrily. "You thought——!"

A large, bass-singing man nearby turned to shush them, but Lucy no longer cared. "Let go! Let go!" she squealed as Alice's sure fingers only clenched the cloak more tightly, so that Lucy nearly choked. With a desperate gesture, she clawed at the fastenings. One button burst. Another, and another. The cloak fell away and was left in Alice's hand. Free at last! Lucy swivelled on her heels and began to run faster than she had ever run in her life before. Along the gutter, down a side-turning, across a cobbled road. Behind her she could hear another pair of pounding feet. She did not have to look round to know whose they were. Faster, faster she ran. Faster too followed Alice's neat black boots.

The echoes of 'Silent Night' were fainter now, but Alice's voice was, though breathless, loud. "Come back! Come back!"

Lucy, still afraid and confused, knew only that for some reason she must make for the Square. It was almost as if it—or somebody in it—were calling her. Her legs ached. Her breath came in painful gasps which made puffs on the cold night air. Alice's legs were longer than her own. She had to keep on, on. . .

"If you leave me, I'll come after you!"

Lucy's heart banged. Another corner then another, and then relief! as she recognised the Square. To be sure a horse-drawn cab trotted down one side of it, and the gas-lights gleamed palely on to cobbles, but Alice was almost upon her, and this place seemed to mean a kind of safety.

Splash! Lucy's right foot landed in an icy puddle. Splash! Splash! She heard Alice's only seconds afterwards. She glanced down briefly as she fled and saw her reflection in the broad puddle, legs racing, hair streaming against the bright rectangle of the electric lamp on the kerb.

The electric lamp!

She hardly dared believe it. Her panicking feet continued to carry her swiftly through the gates ahead and up the short curved drive. There were no footsteps behind her now, though she thought she heard the echo of a sad and angry voice calling. "Come back! Come back!"

There was a violent pounding in her throat as she flung herself towards the porch where Rachel was waiting to meet her.

* * *

"I'm sorry. I truly am."

"Yes, Lucy, we realise that. But you must see that we want to know where you went."

"Out," said Lucy once more.

"Gwen asked you 'Where?'" Her uncle's voice had a sharp edge to it.

"I can't tell you," said Lucy wretchedly. "I'd like to but I can't."

She seemed to have been shut up with the two of them in the study for hours and hours. Neither the hot drinks, nor their patience had succeeded in warming the icy trickle of fear that Alice's words had given her. 'I'll come after you!' She had never wanted to tell anyone the truth more in her whole life, but if she did, Alice would somehow find out. Then what might she do? Lucy shuddered.

"I'm afraid you may have caught a chill," Aunt Gwen said. "You *were* a loony to go rushing out without anything warm on."

"I had my——yes, I suppose you're right."

"You had——?" Aunt Gwen prompted.

Lucy stared at the floor. Her aunt sighed.

Uncle Peter said, "We were so worried about you that we rang Mr. Thomas."

Lucy looked up in horror. "You shouldn't have done that! Oh you shouldn't have! What did he say?"

"Naturally he was very worried and upset when he heard you were missing. But he said he didn't think you'd have actually run away. You aren't the running away sort, he said."

Lucy's eyes filled with tears. Dear Mr. Thomas. He would say a thing like that. "You must tell him that I haven't. Quickly."

"Of course I already have. While you were having your soup in the kitchen. He said give you his love, and that he was looking forward to a letter from you. Apparently your other one never reached him. So you'd better write again tomorrow. Meanwhile we must get things sorted at this end. While you were out, were you alone?"

"Yes. At least, no. In a way."

Uncle Peter looked steadily at her. "Well, which is it? 'Yes' or 'No'?"

"In a way I was alone, but there were other people there."

"Other people, or one other person?"

"Pete, does it really matter?"

"Let me do the talking a minute, Gwen. Who was it, Lucy?"

She twisted her hands. "I'd like to tell you, but I'm very sorry, I can't."

"Did you promise you wouldn't?" Aunt Gwen asked gently.

Lucy turned to her with gratitude. "Yes."

"Then if you're so good at keeping promises," said her uncle, "perhaps you'll make us one?"

Lucy regarded him warily. "If I can."

"I want you to promise never to go off again without telling us where, and with whom."

Lucy thought fast. She could feel them watching her. Would seeing Alice count as breaking the promise or not? It would depend of course, where. And this she didn't seem to be able to control. "I'll try," she said at last.

"That's not good enough."

"I'm sorry, but it's the best I can do."

Uncle Peter said heavily, "This isn't the end of the matter."

"Yes," said Lucy. "I mean, no." She edged backwards, her hand feeling for the door handle.

"Goodnight, darling," said Aunt Gwen. Lucy stared at her for a brief moment. Aunt Olive had called her 'darling'. Since——then, there had been nobody else who even might. Her eyes brimmed again with tears she didn't want them to see. She ran from the room.

*   *   *

"This won't do, Gwen."

"I know it won't," she agreed miserably. "Where have we gone wrong?"

"Surely we've done our best."

"The children, then?"

"They weren't very clever tonight by their own account, but they've already put up with a good deal. Why not lay some of the blame on Lucy?"

"I don't think she can help being—as she is."

"She can't help having lost her aunt, poor child, or being homeless. But she *can* help sneaking off into the night and then refusing to tell us about it."

"I think she'd like to, but she daren't. Perhaps someone's got some hold over her. Oh, I know it seems ridiculous, but—could she have got in with some local gang of toughs?"

"Hardly, she's been with our own toughs all the time."

"Not on the day they shopped. Rachel told me they all parted company to do secret shopping, and she didn't see Lucy again till lunch time. And it was then she seemed to be in such a state."

"It seems very far-fetched to me. Almost as way out as though her poor old aunt has come back to haunt her."

"I didn't say that, Pete. I said I wondered, from something she said, if Lucy had *thought* she'd seen her. Very different."

"Very. It seems to me that you and Lucy both have too much imagination."

"No one can help that."

"No need to let it get out of hand. Half the time I don't think Lucy knows if she's speaking the truth or not."

His wife was hardly listening. ". . . You'll say this is only imagination too, but the other day the sitting-room door opened quite by itself for a few moments. Then shut again."

"A draught. The catch hadn't shut properly."

"Neither of those things, I'm sure. It happened again in the bedroom later. It seemed quite delibe-rate. It was as if someone were peering into the rooms, looking for——"

"My *dear* Gwen!"

"——something or somebody. And yesterday in

108

Rachel's room I could have sworn I was being watched—from out of the mirror!"

Her husband put an arm round her. "Look, you must realise that the move, the school holidays, Christmas, this wretched child—it's all getting on top of you. If she behaves like this again, she'll have to go."

"You wouldn't send her away?"

"Be reasonable. She's turned out to be a much more devious little character than either of us bargained for. She's got on the wrong side of the children, and they're a pretty tolerant bunch for all their faults. She drove us all half out of our minds tonight —just look at the state you're in now! It seems that trying to take her on is proving too much for us all. Her coming for the holidays was only an experiment, remember. We said we wouldn't keep her if it didn't work out. And it's not going to, is it?"

"I think she's in some kind of trouble. We ought to help her, not turn her away."

"How can we help if she won't let us?"

"But somebody must!"

He sighed heavily. "Bed now, we'll have another think about it in the morning."

But upstairs he could see that his wife was still brooding. Presently she asked with apparent irrelevance: "What were those carol-singers collecting for?"

He was glad to discuss a more sensible subject. "It's a funny thing, but I never caught up with them to find out. By the time I'd got to the road, they'd gone."

"They couldn't have, you went out straight away."

"They must have taken a side-turning, or something. Never mind, we'll ask around tomorrow.

Some one's sure to know ... what was that?" he added sharply.

"What was what?"

"I thought I heard somebody laughing."

His wife raised an eyebrow.

He smiled ruefully, but a little uncertainly. "All right, so it's catching!"

But his wife wasn't laughing at all.

Chapter Eight

So now she knew the secret. It was anything which reflected. A mirror was best because it showed the clearest image, but a copper cauldron would do, a darkened window-pane, even a puddle. Now she could go back to Alice whenever she wanted to. But even as she discovered this she realised she was not sure that she ever wanted to see Alice again. Poor lonely little Alice wanted her so badly and she could be a companion in a way that the cousins never could be. But . . . there were some things about her which were much less comfortable: her slyness, her complete disregard for the truth, her determination to get her own way. Of course it was these qualities which made it possible for Lucy to be accepted by people like her Mademoiselle, and Mrs. Naylor. But when Alice turned, as it were, her weapons against Lucy, it could be very frightening indeed. There was something so ruthless about her that Lucy trembled deep inside herself when even she thought of those intently glittering eyes, the clutching fingers, "I'll make something awful happen to you." Could she? Would she?

Although she had become fond of Alice so quickly, Lucy was not sure. Alice wanted her with her so much that she might do anything . . . For there was no doubt that Alice was, in some curious way, powerful. She must have known, all the time the means by which Lucy could reach, and return from, the past. Did the magic also work in reverse? Lucy was almost sure it did. For in the few days since the carolling she had confirmed her suspicions that Alice could find her way into the present. Not that Lucy had ever actually met her. But there had been strange little happenings. . . . Pattering footsteps in the attic when the whole family was downstairs. The whisk of a pinafore round a passage corner.

One day, Aunt Gwen suddenly discovered that having muddled the dates, she was supposed to be attending two meetings on the same afternoon.

"What can I do?" she wailed.

"Simple. Ring one of them and say you can't make it," Uncle Peter advised calmly. "You can't be in two places at once. Somebody's got to do without you."

As Aunt Gwen sprang off to telephone, Lucy's mind echoed those words with a swift return of foreboding: 'You can't be in two places at once . . .' and she remembered vividly Alice's face as she had said that. 'Somebody's got to do without you,' had been her uncle's reply. Lucy shivered. . . .

Two days after the carol-singing, the longed-for letter from Mr. Thomas did arrive. But now, instead of ripping it open, Lucy was afraid to read the reproaches she knew it must contain. She slipped the letter into her writing case and tried to forget about it.

Ever since Uncle Peter's stern words she had been a little afraid of him, certain that he disliked her. (Not that you could really blame him for that. Her behaviour certainly must have seemed terribly queer.) Then one day, he began to feel more like a friend. He came across her doing nothing in particular, and said, "What about that tour of the house?" and Lucy found herself walking round beside him while he explained things. "Might as well start at the bottom. Here are the basements. We keep them locked up because they are really dreadful, and goodness knows when we shall be able to afford to do anything about them." Lucy walked round the dark, echoing, smelly rooms, one leading out of another. She shivered. "They are rather awful. Were they ever used for anything?"

"My goodness, yes! This was the kitchen. The old range stood in that corner. This was the scullery. There's another down that passage, and this was the room where the unfortunate staff lived and moved and had their being."

"In *here*? But it's so dark!" The only light came from a tiny window high in the wall at pavement level.

"Dark and damp and full of cockroaches no doubt, but that sort of thing was considered good enough for servants in the days when this place was built. Something tells me you're not fond of changes, Lucy, but you must admit that some are for the better. How would you have liked to have been cooped up here, and have had to carry meals and coals and so forth up those stairs all day?"

"Not one bit."

"Nor Gwen. That's why the first thing we did, even before we moved in, was to build on a modern kitchen where the old conservatory used to be."

"Conservatory?"

"A place for flowers. Rather like a greenhouse but larger and more romantic. Full of plants and ferns. The traditional place where gentlemen proposed to

113

young ladies! Come upstairs and I'll show you where it was."

It was an interesting tour. Uncle Peter answered all her questions and patiently explained things. "Yes . . . there used to be a fire-place there and I agree real fires are much nicer; but who wants to clean them out? . . . now *this* picture was painted by a friend of mine. . . ." Hearing the histories of the pictures didn't make Lucy like them any more. But she did see that there were reasons for them being there. "Now let's look at the bedrooms. . . ."

By the time they had been everywhere (even the attics where Lucy got the shivers but managed not to show it) she felt that she had known Uncle Peter a long time. He'd been so kind that for a mad moment, as they stood next to Pegasus, she felt like saying, "Now I can tell *you* something about your house. This attic used to be Flo's—she was the house-maid—bedroom. There was a bed here, and a chair here . . ." and so on, and so on. . . . Would he be fascinated by and grateful for the information? No, much more likely he'd stare at her as if she were out of her mind, or remind her that he'd been relating *facts,* not made-up guesses. It would be no good. Regretfully she gave up the idea as soon as she'd thought of it. Instead she said: "Thank you very much for showing me everything," in her politest voice, then added impulsively, "I am truly sorry about—the other night."

"Sorry enough to explain about it?"

She hung her head.

"I see," said Uncle Peter. "At least, I don't see, but perhaps one day you'll be able to make things clearer. Meanwhile I must warn you that none of our children are allowed to behave like that, and if

114

you're going to stay here there must be no more of such nonsense. Understand?"

Lucy nodded.

"Good. Because the next time will be the last time."

In spite of his sternness, Lucy knew that what he had said was fair. She had truly enjoyed going round the house with him. Perhaps it was this feeling of warmth towards him which gave her the courage she needed to face Alice again. She ran to Rachel's bedroom. It was empty. She walked straight to the mirror. "Alice?" she said into it. "Alice?"

Only her own puzzled reflection looked back. The mirror hadn't worked. Why not? Perhaps the attic one would be better. She tried it, but again nothing happened. At a loss she went downstairs to stare into a glass-topped table, at the rounded kettle, into one of the few glass-covered pictures. Nothing. Had she got it wrong after all? Or had Alice in some mysterious way ceased to exist?

But that night she had a horrible dream. She was running away from some monster that looked like a dragon though Lucy knew it to be Alice. "Don't run! I shall catch you in the end!" roared the dragon, breathing blue smoke and orange flames. "No you won't—I can run faster!" screamed Lucy, not believing it even in her dream. But the dragon answered, "No, I shall win—*I shall win!*" and stretched out a great grey scaly claw to clutch Lucy's shoulder.

"Let go!" she shrieked, struggling.

"It's only me," said Rachel. "Do wake up. You were having a nightmare. Shall I put the light on?"

"No," said Lucy.

"Then I'm going back to my bed, it's freezing. You were talking in your sleep again. 'I can run

115

faster!' you said, terribly fussed. Faster than who, Lucy?"

"Somebody you don't know," she mumbled.

"Was it Alice?" The sound of Lucy's bedclothes moving swiftly gave her away. "You've called out her name in your sleep before. Alice who?"

"I don't know."

"You must if she's a friend."

"She isn't."

"But if you don't know her, how can you dream of her?"

"Why do you ask so many questions?"

"Because I want to know the answers. Do tell, Lucy. You're in an awful mess of some sort, aren't you?" Her voice came comfortingly out of the darkness. She sounded as if she really cared. Lucy was tempted. Rachel might find it easier to believe in Alice than her parents would. But if she told, what would Alice do? With a pang, she realised she had inadvertently told a little already. "How ever dreadful a thing is it's better when you've told somebody," Rachel was urging. "I've got into states, so I know." There was another long pause. "If—if you like," Rachel went on with obvious difficulty, "I'll tell you about them."

Lucy was impressed. She could tell just how much Rachel didn't want to give away her own secrets, yet she would if it would help. Alice, she thought inconsequently, would never have given herself away to anyone unless it were to her own advantage. Gratefully she turned on her side to face Rachel, not in order to hear her confessions, but to say something —anything—to repay her for her generosity. She was searching for the right words when Rachel's voice came again. "And if you could come clean about— everything, it would be a terrific help to us."

116

Lucy froze. "Us?"

"The boys and me. The Old Folk have got it into their heads that you were running away because of things we'd said."

"I see," said Lucy. Disappointment flooded over her.

Rachel hadn't been offering real friendship after all. She only wanted to get herself and her brothers out of trouble.

"You can understand that, can't you?" said Rachel.

"Only too well. But you'll have to sort it out with your own precious parents. I can't help it if they don't believe you."

"But——"

"I don't want to talk about it," said Lucy.

*　　*　　*

"This party," said Aunt Gwen next day. "Have you anything suitable to wear, Lucy?"

"What's suitable?"

Aunt Gwen laughed. "You might well ask! Anything seems to go with your age group. Have you had a word with the others?"

"Not yet."

"Then you should. Ah, here's Rachel. Rachel, come here a minute. What are the girls going to wear at the party?"

Rachel looked vague. "I don't know. Anything."

"What about *you*?"

Rachel hesitated. "Jane's got a marvellous new long dress. All frills and tucks. Victorian-looking."

"That'll suit Jane, but you weren't thinking—— you were! Oh Rachel, why didn't you tell me before? I'd thought it would be jeans and jerseys like last time."

"It can be, easily." Rachel spoke quickly. "But if you hadn't got me anything for Christmas I had wondered if——"

"Darling, you were mad not to have asked before. It's early-closing today, the party's to-morrow—there isn't even time to buy the stuff and run something up. Especially as there are two of you."

"Never mind. It doesn't matter a bit. I'll wear that blue thing I had last year. It just fits me."

"And you, Lucy?"

"I've got my red woollen dress, if that'll do."

Aunt Gwen bit the end of her biro. Suddenly her face brightened. "'Victorian' you said. Those two trunks in the attic your father said we weren't to touch, have been there since the year dot. If there were clothes in them they *might* be—— In fact," she looked very guilty, "I *know* they're Victorian because I couldn't resist a peek!"

"Traitor!" said Rachel.

"I know, darling. But only one of them. *Clothes!* —you must see—I couldn't resist costumes—the other's much too heavy."

"Victorian clothes! But Dad said——"

"We've a very special reason, haven't we? I'm sure he'd understand. Let's go *now*, this minute!"

It was strange to be in the attic with other people again. Lucy looked nervously round her. She was not sure, for some reason she could not have explained, that she wanted to look inside the trunk. But Aunt Gwen and Rachel were already undoing the strap round it—creaking open the lid. . . .

"Hurry! Hurry!" Rachel was impatient.

"The one thing we mustn't do," said her mother. "These things may be dropping to bits with age. We must be very careful."

After the first layer of crackling tissue paper there

was a heavy black frock, greenish with age. "For an adult," Aunt Gwen murmured. "Bombazine. Probably mourning, and worn with jet. Well, neither of you want that for a start. Lay it down carefully."

Next came a tartan mantle, an elaborate petticoat, a green checked woollen frock. . . .

"I *said* you could wear it!"

"What?" Lucy asked Rachel.

Rachel looked blank. "I didn't say anything."

"Oh look!" Aunt Gwen was unfolding a pink dress. The bodice was a little row of pleats. The sleeves were puffed. It was trimmed with a narrow edging of lace, which had once been white but was now a yellowish colour.

"I saw one just like that in a shop window the other day! And *what* a price!"

Lucy said nothing. She had seen one just like it the other day too, but not in a shop window. . . . She heard a small chuckle behind her. This time she knew it wasn't Rachel.

"It really is enchanting," said Aunt Gwen, holding up the dress. "It looks in wonderfully good condition too, considering. Would either of you like to try it on?"

"It's too big for me," Lucy said quickly.

Her aunt eyed her. "You may be right. But—is anything the matter?"

"No thank you," said Lucy with difficulty. But the sight and sound of those familiar clothes, the knowledge that Alice was watching, was making her hot and cold in turns.

Aunt Gwen frowned, but merely helped Rachel into the pink dress and struggled with the stiff hooks and eyes at the back.

"There!" she said, when she'd finished. "Don't worry about the lace. We can easily replace it. I've got some downstairs which will do beautifully. This dress is prettier than anything out of a shop-window. There's a glass over there. Prop it up and have a look at yourself."

Lucy held her breath. But when Rachel looked into the glass she only looked pleased and said, "Do you really think I could wear it, Mum? Would Dad mind?"

"I don't think so. And if this kind of thing's being worn as high fashion, it would be an awful waste not to. Now, Lucy, we must find something just as pretty for you."

"It's all right. I don't mind if you don't."

Aunt Gwen looked up in surprise from the trunk. "Surely you'd like one like Rachel's?"

Lucy shook her head. "It doesn't matter. Honestly."

But Aunt Gwen's delving hands had already discovered the one garment which Lucy had most dreaded seeing.

"Oh, lovely!" Rachel exclaimed. "*And* it looks a bit smaller. Do put it on, just to see if it fits."

('But you know it does!') Lucy ignored the voice. "I'd better not." She backed away. "Suppose I split it?"

But she could not resist their kind insistence. Rachel helped her take off her clothes. Aunt Gwen threw the suffocating skirt of Alice's once-white, now cream, party dress over her head. They pulled, tugged, straightened. The familiar folds settled round her as if she had worn it only a few days ago. (Well, hadn't she?) Lucy began to feel dizzy.

"It's a bit loose round the waist." Rachel bunched it round her.

"It's supposed to have a sash," Lucy said faintly.

Aunt Gwen had already found one. "Here it is!

Blue silk. Let me put it on for you. Isn't that perfect, Rachel? Don't worry about its musty smell. We'll hang both dresses out for a good airing. Have a look at yourself, Lucy."

"No," she whispered. "I don't want to."

'Yes you do,' came the voice. 'You know you do. Just *one* look. . . .'

"I shan't!" cried Lucy loudly, and everything went black . . .

"Quick, open the window! It's all right, Lucy. Sit down and put your head between your knees. . . ." They were all concern. Rachel was sent for a glass of water. While she was gone, and as soon as Lucy seemed a little better, her aunt asked. "Is this how you felt that day in the spare-room?"

Lucy nodded. "Yes. Better now, though." But she wasn't, and she knew that Aunt Gwen knew it as she made tactful excuses about it being so stuffy in the attic that anyone might feel faint. She gathered up the two dresses and took them downstairs. It had been assumed the girls would wear them. For the rest of the day Lucy fretted about this. The thought of actually *wearing* Alice's dress. . . . Food made her feel sick. She jumped if anyone spoke to her. She knew she was behaving strangely but she couldn't help it.

It was Bill who—to be fair—didn't know she was nearby when he spoke, and said the thing which hurt: "Loony Lucy *would* be in one of her worst moods just before the party. Let's hope she brightens up before people get here or what on earth will they think!"

She didn't hear Patrick's sharp reproof, or Rachel's anxious shushing. She was already running upstairs as fast as she could. 'Loony Lucy'—oh, how cruel!

121

Without giving herself time to think she dashed to the attic glass. "Alice, they're being *horrid!*"

"I know," said Alice breathlessly in Flo's bedroom. "My goodness, you did come quickly that time! I told you they were. You don't belong with them at all. You belong with me. Come down to the schoolroom, it's too cold for anything up here. You'll have to change, too, in case Mademoiselle sees you."

Lucy looked down at herself, already surprised by her jeans. "Poor Flo has to sleep up here," she pointed out.

"Maids don't mind the cold," Alice said without feeling. "They get used to it. They have to."

"But it seems dreadful that——" Lucy began, but before they had reached the bottom of the stairs she had forgotten what was so dreadful. Alice swept her into the schoolroom and shut the door. "I must say, Lucy," she said petulantly, "it was too bad of you not to have come for such a long time. You might have thought of *me* instead of enjoying yourself with —whoever those people are all over my house——"

Less hazy than usual, Lucy found she was able to reply. "I wasn't enjoying myself. And what do you know about the other people?"

"I don't want to talk about it."

"But I do. And don't say that want must be my master, because this matters." Even as memory slipped from her she felt that it did.

"It matters to me, too," said Alice. "All I know is you're never here for very long when you do come, so do stop being disagreeable. There's so much I want to tell you. Such extraordinary things! A letter came from Mademoiselle. She wouldn't tell me what was in it but I know it was from Mama because I saw the writing after she had put it in a drawer. She thought I didn't know where she had hidden it, but

I did because I watched specially. I couldn't read it though, because I heard her coming back just at the wrong moment—*So* vexing!"

"Alice!"

"—don't interrupt—from a tremendous talk downstairs with Cook and Flo. She wouldn't tell me what about, but she said there would be a lovely surprise soon. I thought perhaps she was leaving (that would have been a lovely surprise!) because I saw her sorting out her clothes, through a crack in the door."

"That was spying! You really——"

"I do wish you'd be quiet. Later I heard Flo wailing, and Cook was in a cross-patch mood because instead of being kind she said, 'Give over, do, and get on with breaking those eggs for the trifle!' That's for my birthday party tomorrow, don't forget you promised you'd come."

"I didn't *promise*."

"But I expect you'll want to. But what can it all mean, Lucy? And Mademoiselle made me fit on all my clothes yesterday to see which still fitted me. And which toys and books I have finished with and will give away to poor children. So stupid, anyone knows poor children can't read. But there is a secret going on, and they won't tell me!" Alice actually stamped. "Who did I see letting you try on my white frock?" she demanded petulantly. "Or is that a secret too?"

"No, that was my Aunt Gwen," said Lucy surprising herself. How could she remember Aunt Gwen when she was with Alice? "She's very kind. She wants me to live with her."

"No she doesn't," said Alice swiftly. "She has her own children—she doesn't need you—she'd like to find you a kind home somewhere else——"

"That's not true!" Somehow Lucy was sure she was right. She took a step back from Alice.

But she was working herself into one of her rages. "Yes, it is! You don't belong with *them*—I shan't let you stay there—you shan't!"

Lucy took another step away. She wished, suddenly, her cousins were here. Alice was becoming frightening. She was now so angry she forgot to be careful of what she said. "I know what it is: you like *that other one* better than me!"

"W-what 'other one'?"

"That *girl* who put on my pink dress without me saying she could. The one that cried when she thought you'd run away. You didn't know that, did you?"

"I know one thing," Lucy broke in. "I'm going back. Now." For some odd reason she was sure she could. She looked quickly. A glass-covered picture of a stag on a moor hung over the bookcase. The sunlight falling sideways on it threw back a reflection that was a mixture of the moorland scene . . . Alice shouting silently . . . a cracked wall . . . a dust-sheet draped over a cupboard . . .

"Hello?" Aunt Gwen looked up in surprise from scraping the spare-room walls. "I didn't hear you come in!"

"I-I'm sorry if I frightened you."

"It's you that looks frightened. What have you been doing?"

"N-nothing much." She was dizzy with the quick change of scene. Aunt Gwen was watching her. "Lucy my love——"

But at the same time another voice cried "Lucy!" from a long way away.

Lucy saw Aunt Gwen's face go cream-coloured. "Did you hear anything, Lucy?"

She was almost brave enough to admit she had. Almost. But not quite. "Only somebody calling me from downstairs, I think. Shall I go and see what they want?"

Without waiting for an answer she ran into the passage.

"Lucy!" came the call again. And it did not belong to anyone in her family. Nor was it from downstairs. Aunt Gwen looked fearfully round the spare-room.

"Lucy . . ." Had the cry come again, or was she imagining it? The scraper clattered from her hand. "Good Lord deliver us," she murmured.

Chapter Nine

IT was on the morning of the party that the first accident nearly happened. Lucy had escaped from the hurly-burly below to the peace of the attic. She now knelt on the low sill to throw open the little window. Knife-sharp winter air rushed in to the stuffy room. Beneath her lay the crisp silvered grass of the square, for there had been a sharp frost in the night. Although there was no wind, the window swung slightly on its hinges causing a glint of sun to catch the glass. Lucy looked quickly away. She was careful to avoid anything which could reflect, just in case. Two boys on bicycles rode madly round the square and stopped at the house. They staggered up the short curved drive carrying armfuls of something heavy. Records for the dreaded party, guessed Lucy, and—'I wonder what Alice's own party will be like?'

No sooner had the idle thought occurred to her than her knees somehow slid from under her. With a gasp she fell forward. She grabbed at the latch for support, but, unsecured, it slid from her grasp as the window moved quietly open as if to ease her way through the frame. For one giddy moment Lucy thought she was going to plunge downwards. . . .

Then someone was dragging her strongly back from the sill.

"Idiot!" said Rachel. "What are you doing hanging out of windows? You might have fallen!"

Lucy huddled, panting on the floor. "Yes," she said thoughtfully. "I might have. Easily."

Rachel seemed exasperated. "Well, don't just sit there! There are hundreds of things to do downstairs. . . ."

There'd been something about that stumble. "How did you know I was up here?" asked Lucy.

"You always are when you want to get away from us, which is nearly all the time," said Rachel.

"There wasn't—there wasn't anyone else in here when you arrived, was there?"

"Anyone else? Who could there be? You were quite alone, looking as if you were just taking a nose dive out of the window."

"That's how it felt," said Lucy, shuddering.

"We'll shut the window," said Rachel, and did so. "Now come downstairs with me." She was oddly bossy, and did not leave Lucy before ushering her firmly into the kitchen to help her mother.

*　　*　　*

"But I tell you, I saw her. She was leaning right out and then she gave a sort of lurch. If I hadn't been there . . ."

"Nonsense," said Patrick. "She's not that daft."

"Sometimes I wonder," said Bill.

"I think you ought to tell the Old Folk," said Patrick.

"Then at least they can't say we kept anything from them," Bill agreed.

Rachel turned furiously on him. "Can't you see

it's more important than that? She's absolutely miserable, I'm sure of it."

"She's an absolute nuisance."

"Patrick, make him see sense."

"I'm not sure that I see it myself," Patrick admitted. "If she'd tried to get on with us seeing as how we're her last chance. But it seems that she thinks anything else would be better than staying here."

"Anything?"

"No. Yes. I'm not sure."

"I'll tell them now. No, it'll have to be just Dad, because Lucy's in the kitchen with Mum."

*   *   *

Lucy was ironing the tiny tucks around the bodice of the pink dress that Rachel was to wear. Aunt Gwen was full of admiration for her patience. "You're going to make someone a wonderful wife one day, Lucy. You really enjoy all the housewifey things, don't you?"

Lucy flushed. "I don't see what's wrong with that."

"Wrong with it? I think it's wonderful. I only wish I did. My mother did try to get me organised without much success. I was too much of a career girl to bother to listen."

Lucy turned the dress carefully on the ironing board. "That's one thing I won't be, anyway. A career girl."

"But you'll have to do something, won't you? Everyone does these days."

"Patrick says a woman's place is in the home."

Aunt Gwen laughed. "Patrick only says that to annoy Rachel 'because he knows it teases'. A woman's place is where she's needed most. When there's a family to bring up, it's often in the home. There is such a thing as earning one's living, you know. Have you never thought about that?''

"No," said Lucy bending low over her ironing.

Aunt Gwen spread some little wooden bowls on the table. "I expect your Aunt Olive talked to you about it sometimes?''

"Never," said Lucy firmly. "Nor schools, nor exams. We didn't even think about things like that."

"Well it's time you thought about them now. Do you realise that term begins soon after Christmas and we haven't made any definite plans about your school yet?''

At the word 'school' a wisp of the old grey fog appeared. "Aunt Gwen, do I *have* to go to school?''

"Certainly."

The nose of the iron encountered the puffs of the sleeve. In—out—in—out. "W-what school would it be?''

Aunt Gwen began to slit open packets of crisps and distribute them among the bowls. "You know the answer to that one—Patrick and Rachel's, if you're here with us."

'If.' Lucy bent low over the ironing-board. "I might not be?''

Aunt Gwen's voice was very matter-of-fact. "That's another thing we shall have to decide, isn't it, Lucy?''

The dress was nearly finished. Lucy turned it over to make sure there were no creases she had missed out. "If I wasn't here, where would I be?''

"I'm not quite sure. Uncle Peter and your nice Mr. Thomas and the lawyer would sort something out. You'd be looked after."

"You mean you'd find me 'a nice kind home' somewhere else?''

"I'm sure that could be managed, but of course we hope you'll stay in the family where you belong."

"But you don't belong, do you?" asked a faint voice which only Lucy heard.

"I don't think that they think I belong."

"They?"

"Your children."

Aunt Gwen hesitated only a moment. "I don't think they feel they know you very well yet. You aren't a very easy person to know."

Lucy gulped. "What about Uncle Peter?"

"He's very fond of you already. But worried because he doesn't think you're happy. And neither do I."

"I didn't run away," said Lucy.

"There are different ways of running away, aren't there?"

"There!" said Lucy, carefully laying the pink dress beside the white one already finished, on the table. "I'll take them up to the airing cupboard, shall I?"

"Yes do, darling, presently. But about running away. Have you ever thought that not facing up to things is a kind of running away too?"

"I don't know what you mean."

"I think you do. Just like I'm not very good at cooking and housework and remembering Christmas decorations, you're not very good at thinking ahead, are you? If you decide you want to stay here we must all understand each other better."

Lucy picked up the dresses and hung them over her arm.

"You've got nearly all your life to lead, Lucy. Very exciting. You've got to look forward and think about what you're going to do with it. Whoever you're with, or wherever you are, you still have to do that. Everyone has to."

Lucy was at the door. *"Please,* Aunt Gwen, I don't want to talk about it," she said and went upstairs.

*   *   *

By teatime the rugs had been rolled away from the library floor, stacks of records were neatly arranged ready for use, the little bowls filled with nuts, crisps and cheese biscuits. Aunt Gwen was talking persuasively in terms of sandwiches and the children were telling her they didn't want them. Uncle Peter and Bill were checking the white lights on the blue Christmas tree and making sure they had spare bulbs if one went out again. For the others, a partyish feeling began to be evident. Other parties were recalled, jokes made which Lucy didn't understand, people talked about whom she'd never met. As she went upstairs to take a last look at the white dress on the bed, she caught herself wishing that she could be at Alice's party instead of this one.

"And so you shall," said Alice.

Lucy, in the empty room, put her hands over her ears. But the voice went on: "And you see, you're wearing my dress for it, like I hoped. I always get my own way if I want it enough."

"It was Aunt Gwen who thought of the dresses," said Lucy aloud.

"Aunt Gwen is quite good at having ideas put into her head. And this was such a good one. You'll come this evening, won't you? We've got a real tree with candles and we shall play games, the kind that you like, and there will be presents for everybody at the end."

"Go away," said Lucy.

"And a proper supper. Lovely ices and jellies and sugar biscuits. Not horrid little things in bowls."

"I said go away."

131

"I will if you'll promise to come." The voice became wheedling. "*Do* say yes! You know how to now, don't you? So——"

"Go away!" said Lucy.

"Talking to yourself again?" enquired Rachel cheerfully, bouncing into the room. "I say, thanks for ironing my dress. Mum said it took you ages."

"It doesn't matter, I like ironing," was all that Lucy said, but she was glad of Rachel's presence and support. Now that it was two against one, she felt safer. She eyed the dresses one on each bed. "What time does the party start?"

"Not for ages. We're going to have a sort of high tea first, and then get the Old Folk bundled into the den. I expect people will start arriving about eight. Lucy, you will try to like them, won't you? And you won't——" she hesitated.

"——disappear again," Lucy finished for her, "and spoil the party for you."

Rachel reddened. "I didn't mean that exactly. About spoiling the party."

Lucy saw that there were tears in her eyes. She remembered Alice saying 'that girl' had cried. . . . She wanted to say, 'I know you didn't, and I won't leave the house, I promise.' But when she opened her mouth to speak quite different words came out of it. "Yes you did. You'd get into more trouble, wouldn't you? Very vexing for you. That's the only reason you want me to stay."

"Lucy, you're talking awful nonsense. You know you are. I only wanted you to promise, for your own good——"

The distress in her face gave Lucy a curious sense of power.

"Then want must be your master. I'm not going to promise anything," she said, and the tone she used reminded her of Alice's. She wondered if she were wearing Alice's triumphant expression too. She almost looked into the mirror to see, but remembered just in time not to.

Rachel was staring at her as if she were indeed a stranger. Then, without another word, she turned and ran from the room. Lucy, feeling much more herself, looked after her with regret.

"Well done," said Alice.

Lucy snatched up the two dresses from the beds and marched with her eyes shut to the mirror. She hung the curved wire of the hangers over the top frame of it. Now it was impossible to see into the glass.

She left the room and slammed the door hard behind her.

*   *   *

". . . I'm not saying she *is* planning to go, Dad. Just that she wouldn't promise not to."

Her father looked grim. "Oh, she wouldn't, wouldn't she? Thanks for the tip. Anyway don't let it spoil your party for you. We'll keep the necessary eye. Though if she pulls that one on us once again . . ."

"You wouldn't send her away?"

"We'll have no choice, Rachel. She's hardly giving the impression that she wants to stay, is she? Anyhow, that's not your problem."

As they changed, Rachel clearly made an effort to behave as if their previous exchange had never taken place.

"Finding these dresses was an absolute brainwave of Mum's," said Rachel as she put hers on. ('Aunt Gwen is quite good at having ideas put into her head!')

133

"It suits you," Lucy said.

Rachel looked enormously pleased. Strange, really, for someone who seemed to care so little about pretty clothes. "But yours looks better. As if it were made for you. Really, Lucy, you ought to have been born a Victorian girl!" She laughed.

Lucy didn't. "I sometimes wish I had."

Rachel stared at her curiously. "You can't be serious! Why? Victorian girls had a terrible time, shut up with governesses, no school, no plans for their lives—" She stopped, a hot blush crept up her neck.

"It's all right," said Lucy with difficulty. "I know all that's true about me too. But don't you see that's why——"

Rachel went back to her bossy mood. "Listen to me, Lucy my girl. It's no good wishing. Wishing never made anything come true." ('Oh didn't it though?') "You're not a Victorian girl. You live in the seventies. Looking forward to fun, and hard work, and marrying, making things happen—or you should be." She paused and then went on, "Is that why you don't like it with us? Because we keep talking about what's going to happen, and you don't like any of it?"

Lucy avoided a direct answer. "I think it might have been rather nice to be a Victorian girl. You didn't have to think about a job or a career. You just got married."

"Or you didn't," Rachel pointed out sagely. "And then what? You became a maiden aunt, and spent the rest of your life running round everyone else. No thank you. But I must say you look the part exactly. Everyone will think you look awfully pretty in that dress. Lucy, do jolly up a bit and try to enjoy yourself tonight. You could, you know, if you made up your mind to. Don't you like parties?"

"Some," said Lucy cautiously.

From the side of her eye she caught sight of a slender shape laughing quietly from the mirror.

And it wasn't Rachel.

* * *

"Hello. How's life?"

"Great. Did you bring that LP?"

"Yes. I've put it with the others."

"Thanks. Lucy, meet Mike. Lucy's our cousin."

"Hello, Lucy."

"How do you do?" said Lucy primly.

"She's staying here for the holidays," said Patrick.

"Terrific. You don't come from out here then?"

"Er—no."

"Which is your school?"

"You can gossip later," Patrick told them quickly. "There's Marian. Marian, come and meet Lucy, our cousin."

"How do you do?" said Lucy.

"Fantastic dress," said Marian. "Rachel's too. Where did you get them?"

"Well——"

"Don't tell them," said Patrick. "Keep them guessing."

"Rotten beast," Marian said amiably. "Are Sue and Jane here?"

"In the kitchen I think."

"I'll go and have a word. See you, Lucy."

"David, this is Lucy."

"How do you do?"

"Hello." Music started. Patrick had to shout above it. "She's come to stay, but she doesn't know many people."

"We'll soon put that right," said David. "Come on, Lucy."

"I'm afraid I———"

"Get *on* with it!" Patrick urged into her ear, and left them. The music seemed louder and louder. David eyed the glittering blue festoons. "A great house, isn't it? Have you ever been here before?"

"No."

"Pity. Hi Maureen—come and meet Lucy. . . ."

But Lucy had had enough. There were too many strange faces, too many eccentric clothes, everybody knowing each other. She must pause to take a breath. But where? Girls were chattering upstairs in the bedroom. Her uncle and aunt were in the den. The hall was still crowded with new arrivals, but as far as she knew the sitting-room was empty. She paused for a moment outside the door to make sure no one saw her escape, but even in that moment a blast of cold air came as yet another arrival pushed into the hall. The draught tinkled the silver Christmas bells hung over the doorway. For a moment, looking up at them, she thought they must fall, but Bill's drawing-pinning held secure. The bells reflected the hall—but a *different* hall? She heard Patrick's voice approaching. "Joey and Kate, at last! Hang on a minute Kate, I want you to have a word with our cousin———"

Oh no, not again, She *must* get away! Lucy slipped into the drawing room to find it was thronged with gay laughing figures. One of them separated itself from the group and came towards her with eager, outstretched hands.

"I'm *so* glad you could come!" cried Alice.

*　　　*　　　*

"Lucy? Haven't seen her for ages," Bill mouthed

above the music. "She hasn't gone off again, has she?"

"I don't suppose so for a moment," said his mother. "Don't worry, she'll be somewhere about."

"Perhaps in the kitchen. There are some girls in there making a gruesome dip."

But Lucy was not in the kitchen. Rachel frowned when asked about her. "In the library I think. Or wait a minute, did I see her going upstairs?"

"Probably. I'll nip up and have a look."

"Do you want me to hunt round?"

"No, no. What's going on in here?"

"Marian's brother brought over a fabulous recipe from Switzerland. A sort of mess of cheese that you're supposed to dip things into."

"It looks disgusting."

"Yes, doesn't it?" Rachel agreed cheerfully. "Never mind, it's terrific fun to make. Are you sure about Lucy?"

"Quite sure, darling. I just wanted to make sure she was enjoying herself." Her mother withdrew from the kitchen. Outside the door she frowned to herself. Lucy was nowhere upstairs she knew, because she had already searched there, even for some strange reason unknown to herself, in the attic. She returned at last unwillingly to the den.

"Well?" said her husband.

"I can't find her."

"She can't have gone far this time. The moment all the children were here I locked both doors. Look." He held up two keys.

"It was a good idea—but it wouldn't necessarily have prevented her, would it?"

"No, but finding the doors locked would have made her stop and think what she was doing. If she were acting on impulse it might make her change her

137

mind. If it was a deliberately planned escapade to draw attention to herself, she'd go just the same."

"Do you think that's why she vanishes?"

"Possibly. There was that thing about pretending nearly to fall out of the attic window this morning. That could have been another example."

"If you're right she must be feeling terribly left out of things, to act like that."

Uncle Peter sighed. "I'm afraid you're right. Let's have another look for her. I'll come with you."

Chapter Ten

THE party was everything a party should be. Lucy had not enjoyed herself so much for a long time. At first shyness, even an unexplained sense of guilt, had made her feel ill at ease. But everyone was so kind that she soon felt more and more at home. The games they played were the ones she had heard Aunt Olive describe; charades, 'Cobbler Cobbler', hunt the thimble. They were silly, childish games, but at a party silly childish games were what one should play. The skirts swished, sashes floated and the little girls' dancing feet ran lightly over the shining floor. The boys joined in with everything, hardly teasing the girls at all. Mademoiselle, with three other governesses to keep her company, nodded and smiled from her corner. Alice, in her new white dress dotted with pink rosebuds, was at her most charming. She introduced Lucy to everyone as, "My friend." It was not until Lucy heard her say to another girl, "She is going to come and live with me soon," that she had to protest, though laughing.

"Now Alice, you know that's not true!"

Alice opened her eyes very wide. "But it is. I've planned it all." She lowered her voice to her companion. "It's still a secret really, but it will happen, you see. Lucy isn't happy at—where she lives."

"What fun you'll have," said the girl. "Just the two of you."

"Yes," said Alice. "Just the two of us, for ever and ever!"

Why were her gay and foolish remarks suddenly unnerving?

After the other girl had moved away, Lucy spoke quite crossly to Alice. "You shouldn't say things like that. I told you that I can't be in two places at once."

For an instant the old sly expression flittered across Alice's pink excited face. "Yes," she agreed. "I've thought of that."

Lucy caught her breath sharply. "I think I'd like to go back."

Alice caught at her hand, in her old impetuous way, "You can't, not now. It's supper-time, and nobody goes until after supper. It simply isn't good manners." She ran to Mademoiselle with Lucy's hand still in hers. "Can we have supper now?" she whispered urgently.

"Suppair? I think, yes? We are ready?" Mademoiselle smiled, and stood up, and clapped her hands. "Now we will have the grand march. And after we have been three times round the room we will march to the supper, yes?"

One of the governesses went to the piano and struck up a loud marching tune. "Take ze partners, please!"

"Lucy will be my partner," said Alice quickly.

Mademoiselle was shocked. "No, no, you should have ze boy for ze partner."

"I want Lucy," Alice said stubbornly, her fingers digging into Lucy's wrist.

140

"I don't want to stay with you," Lucy said suddenly. "I won't!"

"Girls, girls!" cried Mademoiselle.

A round gilt mirror winked cheerfully over the mantelpiece. Lucy was so close, that Alice could not prevent her looking into it, though she tried.

"Don't! You mustn't! Come and have something to eat, something to eat . . . to eat . . ." Her voice faded.

*   *   *

"Hello Lucy!" said Patrick, putting his head round the sitting room door. "Come and have something to eat."

Lucy actually shook her head slightly, she felt so dazed.

"We couldn't think where you'd got to," said Patrick. "The Old Folk are in a fuss again. You are an idiot to keep wandering off. Come and have some dip."

"Some what?"

He showed her what he meant in the kitchen.

"But *what is* it?" asked Lucy.

Mike peered into the bowl Patrick was offering her. "You might well ask. My mother polishes furniture with something like that."

"Don't be so revolting, you haven't even tasted it yet," Rachel accused him.

"As long as it's not like that stuff they put on the salad at school!"

"Even the teachers think that's poison. Did you hear what old Ackerman called it? He actually said . . ."

And away they went about school again. Athletic competitions . . . mountains of prep . . . the fierce maths master . . . house matches . . . it sounded dreadful.

"Any more crisps anybody?" Rachel asked, "Or shall we dance?"

Somebody put on a record. Everybody began moving rhythmically. Jerking about. Looking stupid. Not at all like the proper dancing she had seen earlier.

"Dance, Lucy?" Mike was holding out his hand to her.

She backed away. "I can't do this."

"Nonsense, anyone can. I'll show you."

"No thank you."

"It's not difficult, honestly."

She shook her head. Alice was right. She didn't belong here. She never had, and she never would. "Back in a moment," she muttered, and ran to the sitting-room. This time she made straight for the round mirror over the mantelpiece but of course it wasn't there. Instead hung an oil painting her uncle much admired.

"Bother!" said Lucy. She looked swiftly around the room. She was getting practised now. The coffee table, of course. She hung over its smooth glassy surface. "You were right, Alice."

"Of course I was, you silly goose." Alice tucked her arm affectionately through Lucy's. "I can't think why you ever went off like that. You missed a most lovely supper and we're all full up to here." She put the edge of her hand under her chin. "We're going to have quiet games now."

Lucy was glad enough to have quiet games, although she knew vaguely that she should not be there. Paper and pencils were passed round, and everyone was asked to write down a list; a mountain, a flower, a river, a girl's name. Then someone would

142

choose a letter . . . She and Aunt Olive had often played this game together. She forgot about hazy doubts. She forgot about everything except what she was doing. Time raced by. . . .

*　　*　　*

". . . And there she was. Having supper with the rest of them. Large as life."

"And twice as natural," added her husband.

"I wouldn't say that. She never looks quite natural, poor little thing. But Pete, where *could* she have been? We searched everywhere."

"We couldn't have. She'll have found a hiding place of her own somewhere. Don't let's rootle it out. Everybody needs a hiding place." His wife kissed him. "Hey, don't do a thing like that. One of the children might see and be horribly shocked."

"I'm not sure that I care. But you're right about needing somewhere to hide. That's what Lucy needs. We rather swept her off you know, her aunt's death and then the funeral and only a few days and she was here. Everyone needs somewhere to hide from something like that. Just to give them time to get over it."

"The point is, how much time?"

"Never mind that. So long as we know she's safe at the moment."

*　　*　　*

Tum-de-tum-de-tuddledy. Tum-de-tum-de-tuddle-dy! thumped out the pianist energetically, while the dancers bounced up and down the drawing room performing the complicated patterns of Sir Roger de Coverley. Lucy was scarlet in the face and entirely happy. Alice caught her eye and smiled. She smiled back. At that moment Alice, she was certain, was her best friend, and always would be. Tum-de-tum-de-

143

tuddley . . . She was glad she could still remember these steps from the dancing-class days.

At last the party ended. The girls streamed upstairs to put on velvet cloaks, the boys shrugged on their overcoats in the hall. The front door bell rang again and again as whiskered Papas stamped in out of the cold to collect their families.

When the sound of the last cab had rumbled away, and Mademoiselle, having pinched out the candles on the tree, was yawning delicately behind her hand, Lucy realised that it was time for her, too, to leave.

"Thank you, Alice," she said, meaning it. "I wasn't sure if I wanted to come, but it's been lovely."

Alice threw her arms round her. "I told you it would be! And now for the best part of all—talking about it in bed."

"In *bed*?"

Alice opened her eyes very wide. "But of course! It's nearly midnight!"

"But I'm not going to sleep with you."

"Yes you are," said Alice. "I've arranged it with Mademoiselle. Flo's lit the fire in our room and put an extra bed in it. *So* cosy—you'll like that, won't you? We can put the light out, and——"

"Alice, I'm not going to stay the night. I'm going home."

"This *is* your home."

"No it isn't, it's yours, and——"

"Ours," Alice corrected her. "You're going to come and live with me now."

"No——"

"For ever and ever."

"No—no!"

"You know I always get my own way if I want it badly enough." She was wearing her sly expression now. Her eyes glittered from under half-lowered lashes. Lucy backed away apprehensively. Glass. Where was a glass? Or something that would do. . . .

Alice snatched at her shoulders. "Don't keep looking around. You're to listen to me, I say!"

"I won't!" shouted Lucy, wrenching herself free. "Not a word! And you can't make me." Mademoiselle was still in the drawing room. But there would be mirrors in all the bedrooms. Lucy, grabbing her skirts round her, fled up the stairs as fast as she could run.

*　　*　　*

Bill tugged urgently at Patrick's sleeve. "She's done it again!"

General talking had risen to shouting level, heavily backed by music. Patrick had to bend to hear. "Who's done what again?"

"Loony Lucy. She's gone off."

"She'll come back. She's only gone to take another breather."

"Not this time."

"Let's get out of this." Patrick elbowed his way from the room with difficulty. Bill followed. In the hall they could hear each other.

"How d'you mean 'not this time?'"

"I saw her sneak off, so I followed her. She went into the sitting-room."

"Fair enough. What's wrong with that?"

"She never came out again. I know, because I waited outside for ages. Then I thought she must be getting pretty gloomy, all by herself for so long, so I went in." Bill paused. "She wasn't there."

"She must have been."

"No, I looked absolutely everywhere. All of the

145

windows were shut, but one wasn't properly fastened. She must have got out through it."

Patrick whistled. "Stupid young idiot! Rachel had an idea she might do this."

"I know. I wondered if I ought to tell the Old Folk?"

Patrick considered. "Yes, I'm afraid so, but only if we're absolutely certain she's nowhere in the house."

"But how can she be?—She didn't come back through the sitting-room door."

"I suppose she could have changed her mind, crept back in by the window after you'd gone. I know it's only a remote chance, but—you do realise, young Bill, that if she really has vamoosed again, she's got to go?"

"Go? Where?"

"That's just it. There isn't anywhere. It would have to be a Home, or something."

"You mean an orphanage?" Bill looked aghast. "But look here. Dad couldn't possibly—I mean——"

"Have some sense!" said Patrick irritably. "What else is he to do?"

Bill thought for a moment. "You might be right. Perhaps she *did* come back. I'll have a terrific hunt round the house."

"You do that. I'd better go back to the others or I'll be missed. Make it a good search, young Bill, because if she isn't here we shall have to say, and that'll be it."

Bill did make it a good search. Poor old Loony Lucy. After all, people didn't go running off for no reason at all. There'd been a boy at school who'd run away from home four times. It turned out that he had an awful mother who was hardly ever in. And hit him about when she was, and no father at all.

Come to think of it, Lucy hadn't a father *or* a mother. Only his own family. They'd been as decent as possible, though, thought Bill, and then had a nasty twinge of doubt. The Old Folk had done their bit for sure, and Rachel had fallen over herself to try to understand Lucy. Patrick, though a bit old for her, had made allowances but he himself——? He was uncomfortably conscious that he had decided she was a nuisance and a bore . . . and said so . . . and apart from that . . . But you couldn't let a person be sent to an orphanage just because they were a nuisance and a bore . . . and knowing—well, suspecting, it was partly your fault. . . . He didn't really think she was in the house, but if she was, he'd find her. What's more he'd tell her not to be such an idiot, and offer to lend her some books, or—or—something . . . anything to make her feel at home.

While the thoughts buzzed, he covered every inch of the ground floor, having to make excuses to people who asked what he was up to, or where was he off to in such a tear. "Shan't be a minute," he kept saying, and as soon as they'd lost interest in him, looking in quite ridiculous places like under the kitchen table and in the stuffy little coat cupboard, because he had to be *certain*.

Upstairs was easier because there were only stray guests on their way to the bathroom or those two idiots Mark and David playing a private chasing game, thump-thump-thump all over the place. Mark actually hurtled into Bill and they both went flying. They wanted him to join in, but he only said, "In a minute, p'raps," and went on with his hunt as soon as they were out of the way.

"*Lucy!*" he kept calling urgently. "Lucy? If you're there, do *say* something!" Once he actually thought he heard her answer 'You can't make me!'

147

or something stupid like that, but it must have been his imagination because when he flew to the spare room, which is where he'd thought the voice had come from, there was no sign of her.

Then he heard footsteps on the attic stairs, fast thumping ones; but listening carefully as they reached to the top and tore down again, he realised they belonged to two people, one close behind the other. Those mad boys again. All the same it wouldn't have hurt to have a look at the attic, since Lucy often went up there.

Here again, though, he drew a blank, and was just going to return to Patrick with the bad news when a girl careered round the corner of the passage, pulling up short at the sight of him. Bill started in surprise. Surely he'd never seen her before? He didn't remember that flowery dress—rather the same sort of shape as Rachel's and Lucy's—or that mane of hair? Must be a friend of Rachel's who'd arrived late.

"Sorry!" he said, though the near-bump had been her fault rather than his. Her chest was heaving, her face flushed. Perhaps she'd joined the boys' game, though she made no attempt to go on with it now. Just stood looking at him with strangely glittering eyes.

"I'm looking for Lucy," he explained.

She said nothing. Just stared at him.

"Have you seen her?" Still no reply. Just that odd, dark unnerving scrutiny. "It's important," he went on desperately. "Terribly important. She's lost, and I've got to find her. Now. Because if she disappears again, she'll be sent away." Did he see a flicker of triumph cross her face? "Which would be quite wrong," he plunged on, "because Lucy's part of our family and we don't want to let her go." Ridiculous to blurt all this out to a completely strange girl, but there was something about her that seemed to draw unwilling words from him. Not that she looked friendly. Rather the opposite. Her mouth was hard, her eyes half closed. He rather thought she stamped but was never certain. It was at that point that he found he was very cold. His teeth began to chatter a little. From the cold of course, because there was no need to be frightened of a little girl. All the same . . . He looked away involuntarily from that expression of deep dislike, and when he looked back, she'd gone. It took quite an effort to force himself to dart after her, but when he'd rounded the corner there was no sign of her on the landing. Funny. She'd hardly had time to—But now that she had gone Bill again remembered the importance of his search.

"Lucy!" he called, for some reason with more urgency than before.

*   *   *

Alice's bedroom—and then safety. But Lucy had a shock. For when she burst into the room it was to find the mirror had been turned to the wall. So had all the pictures. She looked wildly round for something shining. Nothing.

"You're *going* to stay!" she heard Alice call. She ran into the schoolroom. Here, too, every picture was twisted back to front on its cords. "You can't make me!" she called back, but with the edge of despair in her voice, for clever Alice had anticipated her wish to escape.

Where next? Flo's bedroom. She *knew* there was a mirror there. But as she tore up the attic steps she heard Alice close behind her, and when she got to Flo's bedroom, the mirror was not there. She ran into cook's. No glass.

"You see?" cried Alice appearing triumphantly blocking her way down stairs. Lucy pushed past her and raced down the attic stairs. She heard Alice pounding after her. Downstairs—but here was Mademoiselle carefully putting out the gaslights at the foot of them. Lucy shrank against the wall. Her breath was coming in huge gasps. Her knees trembled. She was trapped, deliberately trapped, by Alice. A huge unreasonable fear filled her. She must escape! She must!

She became aware of voices on the landing behind her. Who could Alice be talking to? The angle of the wall hid the speaker from her. Mademoiselle moved unhurriedly towards her own bedroom. If only she'd be quick, Lucy would have time to get downstairs before Alice caught up with her again. Mademoiselle was at her door now, was turning the handle. Suddenly Lucy stiffened. "Lucy's part of our family and we don't want to let her go!" She heard the words distinctly. And even in her terror she recognised the speaker. Bill! Bill whom she'd always thought could not wait to be rid of her.

As if a spell had been broken her feet leapt again into action. Down the stairs they carried her, into the drawing-room . . . And there was a round clean patch of wallpaper over the mantelpiece where the mirror had been!

"I'm coming!" cried Alice from the hall. Lucy's heart banged. Then she remembered the conservatory. She ran towards the tall windows that led to it, rattled open the curtains that covered it, wrenched at its handles. It stuck. She could hear the swish of Alice's dress as she ran into the room behind her. Quick! There were bolts at the top and bottom of the window. Snick—snick—and a cool waft of mingled scents enveloped her. Ferns brushed her hot face as she rushed through them towards the glass wall from outside which the midnight darkness threw back a strong reflection . . .

* * *

"Goodbye—thanks for coming!" It had been said for the last time. Now there was only the family left to clear the debris and drag itself wearily to bed.

"Where's Lucy?" asked Aunt Gwen, her dustpan in one hand and brush in the other.

Patrick shot Bill a look. The time had come now with a vengeance. But Bill said, "Somewhere about. She'll turn up to help in a minute."

Patrick cornered him privately in the kitchen. "Look here, we've *got* to tell them——"

Their father came in with a tray of glasses to be washed. "That's right, grab a cloth both of you." Rachel was behind him with another tray. She gave her brothers an anxious, questioning look. Aunt Gwen hurried in, turned on the taps so hard that they sprayed everywhere, cursed herself for being careless, and started to wash glasses. "You'd think they'd used about three each——oh, hello, Lucy! Where did you spring from?"

Lucy was too much out of breath to speak. She looked swiftly round as if surprised to find herself in the kitchen. "Sorry, I—I—didn't know you'd started——" She picked up a tea towel and a glass.

"You've been running," said Uncle Peter. "Where have you been?"

"Nowhere," said Lucy. She leaned suddenly against the table.

"Feeling quite well, Lucy?" Aunt Gwen asked.

"Yes thank you." But she didn't. She felt as if in a nightmare when you wanted to run and run but your feet wouldn't take you. Yet there was nothing to run

151

from in this bright warm kitchen filled with people she knew. She held up the glass to see if she had dried it properly. Her tiny figure was reflected in it. Upside down. Yes, that was reasonable. Everything was upside down, even that tiny figure. *And the other one beside it.* A tremor shook her, then a hotness, then a chill. She gasped for breath. With one hand she clutched at the table, the other clenched crushingly round the glass.

"Lucy!" Aunt Gwen rushed towards her. Rachel gave a little cry, Uncle Peter jerked out a chair from under the table. Patrick did something at the basin. . . . They came and went blurrily. Her ears were filled with the sound of mocking laughter, and the blood from her cut hand ran all over the white dress.

Chapter Eleven

"BUT she just scrumpled it up as if it were tissue paper!" Now even Patrick sounded worried.

"She'd had an exhausting evening," said his mother. "She didn't know what she was doing. It could have happened to anyone."

"Is is very bad?" Rachel asked.

"No. It looked much worse than it was. Dr. Brown said she was lucky. If she'd cut a nerve, or an artery . . ."

"She didn't do it on purpose! I'm sure she didn't!"

"Of course not, darling. We all know that. It was just a silly accident. You go upstairs and be with her. Dad's up there now, and I expect she'd like to come down."

"She'd probably rather be left alone."

"Don't you believe it," said her mother. "She wants us more than she lets on."

"Mum," said Patrick, as the door closed behind Rachel, "we're not keeping guard over her, are we?"

"Not exactly. But we don't quite know what she's going to do next."

"So you *do* think she did it on purpose?"

"Not consciously. Dr. Brown says that people under stress can become what's called 'accident prone'. Patrick looked blank. "It means they don't intend things to happen to them but they sort of attract calamity."

Patrick frowned as he thought of all that red blood and Lucy's greenish face. Surely no one could *want* to do that to themselves? "But there was the window business——"

"Another typical example, apparently. Deep inside herself Lucy's dreadfully upset, Patrick. That's what's making her behave so oddly. It's what people mean when they say 'She's not herself.' She's not."

Patrick's frown deepened. "Funny you should put it like that. Rachel said almost the same thing. Mostly Lucy's quiet and—well, a bit dull. Then suddenly she'll come out with something quite nasty. Not the sort of thing you'd expect her to say at all. Almost, Rachel said, as if she'd turned into somebody else!"

His mother gave him a quick look but she only said, "What a mysterious and miserable business it all is. Your father thinks she ought to go away, for a time, at least."

"But where to?"

"There are nursing-homes where people who are" —she hesitated—"disturbed, can go for proper rest and treatment."

"Poor animal. To be bunged off again, so soon."

"But if that's what's best for her, I suppose—And anyway, I thought you were all finding her rather a trial?"

"Not *that* much."

"Here you are!" his father exclaimed, appearing in the doorway. Still gossiping? Come on, bed. And you, Gwen. Anything that's left can be cleared up in the morning."

"We were talking about Lucy."

154

"No doubt. Nobody's discussed anything else for days, it seems to me. I won't have any more of it. My dear girl, have you *seen* yourself lately? You'll be the next to crack up."

"But——"

"No!" said Mr. Long very firmly indeed. "Tell me about her in the morning if you must, but as far as tonight goes, to use a familiar phrase: 'I don't want to talk about it.'"

*   *   *

For once Lucy slept soundly. Nothing—and nobody could penetrate the comforting effects of the pill Doctor Brown had given to help her rest. But in the cold grey morning she stirred uneasily, half awake one minute, dropping off again the next. Tattered dreams troubled her. A frantic, and never-finished chase. A search for—what?

Then her hand started to hurt quite badly. She moaned a little, but at least the throbbing dispelled the dreams. From time to time she was vaguely aware of movement in the room, the door opening and closing quietly, briefly peering faces. "Still a bit dopey," she heard a voice whisper, "better leave her a bit longer . . ."

Later she saw Aunt Gwen quite clearly. "How do you feel, darling?"

"I'm not sure," said Lucy.

Aunt Gwen said she might know better after a wash and some breakfast. The wash was welcome, but Lucy must have dozed off again before she'd finished the breakfast (scrambled egg with a spoon) for when she next woke the grey had gone and bright sunlight filled the room.

Rachel crept in. "Sorry, did I wake you? The thing is we're going out. We've got to lug the empty coke bottles back to the shop. Is there anything you'd like?"

"No thank you."

"Gosh, Lucy, you look pretty awful. The boys said to say all the right things for them. What about a magazine? Or chocolate? Or grapes? They're what invalids are supposed to want."

"I'm not an invalid."

"I must say you look like one. All right, we shan't be long. The Old Folk are shut in the den, writing cards like mad. They said to ring this little bell if you want anything." She put the bell on the bed-side table and was gone.

Lucy lay. Sounds of traffic drifted up from beyond the square. Inside the house was silence . . . until the first whisper.

"Lucy?"

She pretended not to hear. The whisper again: "Poor Lucy! Are you listening?"

"No," murmured Lucy, her eyes closed.

"So you are awake! Now listen——"

"I don't want to listen." This was true. She felt warmly wrapped in a cocoon of bedclothes and of kindness. Alice wasn't kind. She thought only of herself. "Go away," said Lucy.

"But I *am* going! This very morning! That was Mademoiselle's surprise. Can you imagine anything so exciting?"

"But where——? I don't understand."

"To a house in the country that Papa and Mama bought as a secret surprise for us all. They're there now, and the boys are coming to it. Mademoiselle has been packing away the things I shan't need to be stored in the attic till later. Poor old Dobbin and old clothes and books and things. Cook and Flo are crying but I think it's wonderful news don't you? I

156

shall have a pony, and—Lucy, are you still listening?"

But Lucy was not. A pleasant muzziness had crept
over her. She sighed, slept. She woke again, not
knowing if she'd been asleep a minute or an hour,
Alice's words still insistent in her ears.

"Can't you hear me? Oh, you are vexing! Lucy,
this is important. I'm going away."

"I hope you have a lovely time, Alice," murmured
Lucy in a slurry voice.

"So you *can* hear me!" Alice, who had sounded a
little tearful, at once became brisker. "I *shall* have a
lovely time. I've arranged all that. It's nearly perfect
isn't it? But Lucy, one thing: we must say goodbye.
After all, you are my very best friend—the only
person I have."

"Not now. You've got a family again, remember.
And I think I'm going to have one too."

"Oh, *them!*" Alice's voice was scornful, before
quickly changing back to its wheedling tone. "But
families aren't the same as best friends, are they?
Someone to do things with always. Please come and
see me just once more. For the last time." She gave a
little sob. "You wouldn't be so *cruel*——"

Alice had never cried before. Lucy was used to
seeing her raging and threatening—but not crying.
In her mind's eye she could see those sharp little
black eyes softened by tears. Poor Alice. Lucy felt a
stirring of pity.

"I know you'll come. And Lucy, I'm sorry I played
a trick on you last night. The looking-glasses and—
and—things. I *so* wanted you to stay!"

Lucy remembered the terrifying panic of no-
escape. She was not going through that again, however
much Alice wept. In fact, on second thoughts——

"No! No! You *must* come!" cried Alice. "Don't

157

you see how important it is? I'm going *away*, I tell you! You'll never see me again!"

There was, Lucy found guiltily, an enormous comfort in that thought. One more meeting, and then she could feel safe. She need tell no more lies. She'd be free to start again. No more Alice. It was too much of a temptation.

"Oh, all right," she agreed, in spite of herself. Anything would be better than this endless cajoling.

"Dearest Lucy! I knew you'd do it! But no one must hear us—and they're getting rather good at that. We must meet outside."

"Outside? But I'm not supposed to get out of bed."

"Never mind what you're supposed to do!" All the old impatience had returned now that Alice was getting her own way. "Creep out the back way. I'll meet you in the garden square."

"But——"

"I must go now. The cab's all packed up. Mademoiselle will be here soon. Hurry, Lucy, or it will be too late. Hurry. . . ."

For several minutes Lucy continued to lie in bed. The very thought of getting up and dressing was exhausting. Then she thought of Alice waiting in the garden. It would be unkind not to go. And besides, there was a reward . . .

Dressing was slow and difficult. Her hand throbbed and her head swam. The bandages would not be squeezed through the sleeve of her jersey, so she had to leave it swinging empty. When she was ready she had to sit on the bed and pant a little. Then she inched open the door. It would certainly be dreadful if the Old Folk discovered her escaping. No one could blame them for being terribly angry, and for

158

not understanding that in a strange way she was not going from them, but *towards* them.

The den door was closed. The murmuring voices from behind it droned on as she tip-toed past and out of the back door. The cold was bitingly fierce. Icicles spiked down from the porch. The milk on the step had pushed its creamy head over the top of the bottles. Starlings fluffled in huddles on the telephone wire. The air sliced at her hot cheeks.

Lucy rounded the house and tottered cautiously down the drive, finding it difficult to keep her balance with one arm pinned to her side. The pavement was as slippery as glass. Even the blue-scored road where cars had passed was difficult to cross. In the garden in the square the grass crunched like sugar, the lily-pond lay round and black under a layer of ice.

Lucy looked round for Alice but there was no sign of her. Funny. She'd sounded so urgent. Perhaps she had gone already? Lucy waited one shivery minute. Two. It was so cold that she began to walk carefully up and down. Her hand ached and her head ached. She wished she was back in bed.

"No, no!" said Alice. "Not till we've said good-bye."

"But where are you?" Lucy looked round in bewilderment.

"Come to the pool."

The stones which bordered it were coated with ice. Alice laughed her most mischievous laugh. "Can't you see me? Look at the ice, stupid!"

Staring into the depths of the pool Lucy could at first see only silvery creases where the wind had riffled the surface as it froze.

"Nearer the middle is smoother," said Alice.

159

"Stand on the very edge and you'll be able to see better."

"It's so slippery," Lucy said nervously.

"Never mind . . . that's better. . . . Lean over . . . now I can just see you!"

And Lucy could just see Alice in the black depth of the pond, wearing her caped coat, a tammy and expression of glee.

"Come here—I've got a surprise for you!"

"I can't."

"There's no such word as can't. Step on to the ice."

"I'm not sure it'll bear me."

"Nonsense, it would bear a carriage and pair."

Doubtfully, Lucy slid one foot on to the ice.

"Hurry!" Alice urged once more.

But Lucy couldn't hurry. Not only was she nervous of the ice, but another kind of fear also held her back. She was beginning to know Alice too well to trust that determined expression. She glanced behind her at the safety of the frosted grass.

"One step more," persuaded Alice, "that's right . . . and another . . ."

A sharp crack rang out across the quiet square.

"Oh!" cried Lucy, panic-stricken. "It's break-ing——!"

"That's right," Alice crowed. "You're going to come through. That's the secret, Lucy! *You're coming with me!*"

C-r-r-ack! went the ice again.

"That will make it quite perfect, you see? I plan-ned it all——"

Lucy tried to swivel. One foot shot from under her. She fell heavily on to a knee. As she crashed down, she tried automatically to fling out a hand. The wrong hand. She screamed.

"... *they* were too clever the other times, but now it's too late ..."

Lucy tried to crawl but the ice was splitting from under her. She glimpsed Alice's triumphant face being shattered by the disintegrating reflection, and faintly heard her cry out: "Come to me—I'll hold you!" as she lifted up her arms towards her. Then there was only one last shriek of laughter—no more Alice—no more ice—just heaving icy water. Before Lucy herself could cry out she was in it. The shock made her gasp. The dirty water rushed into her mouth. Choking, she tried to strike out with her arms, but one was useless. Worst of all, another pair of arms was twining round her legs, tightening their grip, dragging her downward, downwards.

"Alice! Let go!" But Lucy didn't know if she shrieked the words aloud or only inside her head.

The grip tightened and she was pulled beneath the water. Dark ... a pain in her chest ... in her ears ... she tried to kick her legs free, thrashed wildly with her one arm ... glimpsed the sky, and was able to take one choking breath before the water closed again over her head. She was lost, and she knew it. ...

Strong hands grabbed at her water-logged shoulders, hauled under her arms. The sky again. Air, lovely air. Somebody crying. Somebody else growling: "Shut up, and give me a hand." The drag of those fierce invisible hands under the water. The edge of the pool bruised her shoulder, dug into her hip. Hard ground. Icy air all round her. A sudden feeling she was going to be sick. A preliminary shuddering gasp ...

"Patrick, I don't think she *is* drowned!"

"I told you so. Turn her head to one side. Help

161

me get my coat under her. Bill, nip in and tell the Old Folk. . . ."

The icy stones grazing her face . . . being covered . . . lifted . . . carried . . .

She knew no more.

*   *   *

Doctor Brown listened gravely, then shook his head. "I'm very sorry to hear this. It's more serious than I'd thought———"

"Then she needs treatment."

The doctor smiled. "Certainly, Mr. Long. And the best treatment for a lonely imaginative child is the warmth of a family round her. No treatment like it. Never has been and never will be."

"I dare say you're right. But I have to consider my own family as well. The children had a nasty shock this morning, and as for Gwen, she's hardly had a moment's peace of mind since the child arrived." He glanced towards his wife as she spoke.

"That's true," she admitted, "but not so much because of the way she behaves, as *why*———"

"Fairly obvious on the face of it," Doctor Brown said. "Shock, repressed grief, insecurity . . . If she could express her feelings it would be the greatest possible help. I wish you'd try to get her to talk. If not about her specific troubles, then about anything at all."

"We have tried—all of us."

"I'm sure you have. Don't think I'm blaming you in any way. But perhaps you could make Christmas the occasion for even more effort? And another thing: I know she's only here on a temporary basis; so does Lucy. Mr. Long, if she shows signs of settling down in a normal healthy way with you, are you still willing to have her?"

162

"Of course. We said that from the start. *If* she wants to join the family."

"Good. Then perhaps you could take it for granted when you speak to her, that she's here for always. Not because she has nowhere else to go, but *because you want her*."

"But we do, don't we, Pete?"

He sighed. "Of course we do. All things being equal, which at the moment they certainly aren't. I do wish you wouldn't make me sound the villain of the piece. I could get very fond of the child if she'd give one the chance."

"It's you who are going to give her the chance," said the Doctor. "Do all you can, won't you? Because it might be the chance of a life-time."

* * *

Lucy asleep upstairs knew nothing of this conversation, or of the family conclave which followed it. She woke after tea heavy with unhappiness. She'd gone too far this time. No family could be expected to take responsibility for somebody who'd behaved as she had this morning. Those dreaded 'other arrangements' would have to be made. It was odd to think that a fortnight ago she had been planning to run away. Now she'd give anything to know she could stay. The knowledge that she couldn't made her feel as if a marble were lodged in her chest. Nor could she be sure if the grey fog closing round the darkening window were real, or the same desperate threatening kind which had enveloped her when she had first realised she was homeless.

The door opened. Lucy went rigid under the bedclothes at the thought of Uncle Peter's justifiable anger, or Aunt Gwen's natural disappointment. She didn't know which she dreaded most. Both of them came in. She braced herself.

Uncle Peter—surprisingly—only smiled at her as he snicked on the light and drew the curtains against the winter gloom outside.

"You poor old thing!" said Aunt Gwen. "Lying awake all by yourself. We thought you were still asleep. Pete, give the others a call, would you? Let's get you sitting up—Pete, grab Rachel's pillow to prop her with—that's right—and put the fire on. Have you a bedjacket or something, Lucy? Let me have a look—oh!" For she had swept open the drawers alloted to Lucy and found them all empty. "My dear child, what have you done with your things?"

"They're still in my trunk," said Lucy in a small voice.

"Your trunk?" echoed Uncle Peter.

"I—I thought I might not be staying," Lucy admitted. And then, having got that far, rushed on, "And now I won't be now, will I? After this morning. I'm very sorry about that, I——"

But, astonishingly, they didn't seem to want to hear about the morning. Aunt Gwen seemed much more interested in making her husband help her unpack Lucy's trunk. All the time her voice went on in its usual disconnected way: "... *what* a pretty dress! It ought to be on a hanger, see if Rachel's got a spare one—yes, we were sorry about this morning too—look in the cupboard, then—our fault, one of us ought to have sat with you all the time, pills can have extraordinary side-effects on people—here's a skirt to go next to the dress—only we never thought of you sleep-walking—slips and vests in the middle drawer—lucky thing the others came along just

164

when they did, wasn't it?—handkerchiefs and belts in the top drawer——"

As she rattled on, working like a whirlwind at the same time, Lucy could only lie back among the pillows dumb with surprise. Were there to be no demands for a proper explanation? No 'other arrangements'? (After all they were *un*-packing as hard as they could go.) The grey fog hung uncertainly round her.

Aunt Gwen came to the paintbox ("Oh! How heavenly!"), the writing-case, the mother-of-pearl counters. "Lucy! What beautiful things! You'll want to put them away yourself. Look at this dear little fan—broken, but never mind, I'm sure it can be mended——"

Rachel appeared and saw Lucy sitting up. "Good, you must be better."

"Look!" cried her mother. "Happy Family cards —the original design—*so* much nicer than the modern versions. But we mustn't touch all this——"

"Oh yes. Please do touch," said Lucy, enjoying sharing her treasures for the first time. Patrick and Bill arrived in time to hear their father exclaiming over the chess men. "Quite beautifully done—hand-carved. Much too handsome to be hidden away. We must design a special shelf in your room to display them, Lucy."

"Oh—you haven't told her?" said Bill.

"Not yet they haven't," said Rachel.

"But we may as well now," said Uncle Peter laughing, "since I've let the cat out of the bag. We thought the very best Christmas present we could give you might be your own bedroom," he explained to Lucy.

Everybody joined in with the explaining.

"We'd all have to work like mad to get it done before next term——"

"Mum says she'll help with the curtains and things——"

"And Dad will design it—*not* his usual way, but with your very own old-fashioned furniture if that's what you'd like best——"

"You won't be able to do much with that hand but you could sort of supervise——"

"Would you like that, darling?"

Lucy liked it so much that she found she could say nothing. When she opened her mouth only a kind of croaking came out of it. The marble rose in the throat, and the tears so long uncried now spilled violently down her cheeks. Patrick looked uneasily at Bill who half stood up. Uncle Peter looked at Aunt Gwen who firmly shook her head.

"Have a terrific howl," advised Rachel, "you'll feel wonderful afterwards."

Lucy couldn't have stopped anyhow. But just as she was thinking the whole idea was almost perfect, the phrase reminded her of—of——

"But what about Alice?" she whispered.

Chapter Twelve

THERE was a short silence. Lucy, fumbling for a handkerchief, sensed the others looking at each other. Then Aunt Gwen, settling on Lucy's bed said in a most matter-of-fact way: "Yes, what *about* Alice?"

Lucy looked round. Uncle Peter had sat down. The cousins were sprawled across Rachel's bed. The five faces were all turned towards her, waiting.

And of course she could tell them nothing.

"You've kept her to yourself far too long," Aunt Gwen went on. "I know she doesn't like to be talked about, but she doesn't always play fair herself, does she? So out with it." She made Alice, so frightening and powerful, sound like a naughty little girl of no particular importance. And yet—"Do you *know* her?" Lucy asked in astonishment.

"In a way, yes," said her aunt, as if it didn't much matter one way or the other. "How long have *you* actually known her? Months? Years?"

"Of course not! It was *here* she used to live!"

"How stupid of me—I was forgetting. How did you first meet her?"

"It was—" But she couldn't possibly go on.

"We'll believe you, and we won't laugh," promised Aunt Gwen as if she were a mind-reader.

So at first very slowly and hesitatingly, Lucy began . . .

Soon there was no sound in the room but that of her own voice describing Alice, Mademoiselle, the house as it had been, trying on clothes, the scrap-album, the meeting in the street. . . . The intense interest of her hearers gave her courage. As she told of each incident it became so vivid that she re-lived it. The birthday party, the horrifying excitement of discovering Alice's clothes in the trunk, of actually wearing the white dress, the two parties, ("So that's where she got to!" whispered somebody) then Alice's vicious threat: 'I'll make something awful happen!' Lucy choked on the words. Her free fingers clenched on the eiderdown. Her mouth went dry. "I didn't know just how awful she meant———"

Aunt Gwen took her hand in her own and uncurled the fingers. "Be brave—you've nearly finished —we do so want to hear *everything*. Tell me, how did Alice persuade you to go to the lily pool?"

"She talked to me up here in bed. She sounded so desperate and sad. I didn't want to go, but she said it would be the last time I'd ever see her."

"So you went—and we know the rest."

"But you didn't know how awful it was!" Lucy found she was crying again. "She *knew* the ice would —break—and she kept saying 'one step more'—and pretending to be—and all the time—and I could feel her arms pulling me down—*pulling*—" Her voice dissolved into sobs.

Uncle Peter stood up. "Lucy, I can't tell you how glad I am to have heard all this. And well done for telling us. Now I'm going to get my drawing board and start planning that room of yours." He smiled kindly and left the room.

Patrick glanced in an embarrassed way at Lucy still snuffling into a new handkerchief. "I'll do a bit of scraping to help the good work on." He too was gone.

Lucy looked up, hopelessly blotched, but calmer. "They don't *really* believe me," she said sadly.

"Well *I* do," said Bill. "You see, I think I've met your Alice."

"You *what?*" they all exclaimed.

Bill described his encounter on the landing.

"But darling," said Aunt Gwen at the end. "Why are you so sure it was Alice?"

"There was no one else it could be. And there was something not quite right about her. . . . I felt it at the time . . . and I think she was hunting for Lucy too . . . anyway, don't ask me why but I'm *sure* I'm right. In a way it was me that saved you from her, Lucy, not Patrick at all," Bill finished, pleased with himself. "I held her up long enough to let you get away."

"But you didn't know you were," Rachel put in, jealously. "I think you imagined the whole thing. You made a mistake. You don't know all my friends, and after all, she never *said* anything. I'm sure——"

"One thing *I'm* sure about," Aunt Gwen spoke with great firmness, "is that between the lot of us we've made a mess of this room. Buzz off, you two, while I clear things up a bit."

After they'd gone Aunt Gwen began a great tidy-up. "Look, things are spilling out of your writing case," she said in the course of it. "Oh, here's an unopened letter! Had you forgotten it?"

Lucy flushed. "No. But it came from Mr. Thomas, after Uncle Peter had rung him up, and I knew he'd be—he'd feel that I—anyway, I didn't want to read it. So I put it away and tried not to think about it."

"Now that you know quite well that hiding things and trying not to think about them doesn't help, don't you think you ought to open it?"

A few minutes later Lucy cried: "I *wish* I'd read it before! He wasn't angry at all. He said he's sure I must have had some good reason for doing what I did—and if I'd explain . . . and he says he *knows* I wouldn't let them down . . . and he's been ill, that's why he didn't write sooner . . . and Mrs. Belling's had her baby, a boy, and she'd like me to go and see it while it's still small—may I?—and he sends love from them all——" She found her eyes were wet again. "Do you think I could send him some home-made mince-pies like Aunt Olive always did? He loved them so."

"Of course you must. You are a donkey, Lucy! Do you make a habit of leaving letters unread?"

It was an evening for telling the truth. "Most of the one from you I did," she admitted with shame.

"But Lucy——! Read it at once, you bad girl!"

Now that she knew her aunt's voice so well, she could hear it in every word of the spiky writing, and recognised the well-meant kindness of '. . . and sometimes it's the last straw when people suddenly talk about people who have died, at the wrong moment. So I've warned the children not to mention your Aunt Olive till you do, and we'll leave it to you to make the first move.' And all the time she thought it was because they hadn't cared!

Lucy hugged Aunt Gwen. "I'm sorry. I didn't know you then."

"So is there anything else it would be a good idea to talk about?"

170

"Well—I'd like to find out more about Alice."

"Are you quite sure?"

"Yes. There must be some way of finding out. Because of records of people who used to live in the house? Then we'll remember her as a person and not a ghost. No, don't look like that. It was you who said 'From ghoulies . . .'"

"Because you can be haunted by your inside thoughts, you know."

"She wasn't just an inside thought. She got realer and realer. Didn't she? Some times more real than all of you. Sometimes more real than me!"

"But you'll never see her again."

"Are you sure?"

"Quite, quite sure."

"You mean because she doesn't need me any more?"

"Much more important than that, Lucy. Because *you* don't need *her* any more."

*   *   *

Uncle Peter lay back in his chair in the study, no longer looking at the book in his lap, but staring at nothing in particular. His wife came in.

"You look stunned, darling."

"Aren't you?"

"Rather, yes. But perhaps not so much." She sat in the chair opposite his. "*What* a dreadful story! No wonder the poor child—what *have* you been doing to yourself? Your hands are black and there's a great smudge on your cheek. Grubbing about in the spare-room with the others, I suppose. No wonder she was distraught. That naughty Alice never gave her a moment's peace. Are you listening?"

"As little as possible. I was thinking."

"Me too. Furiously. So many things fit together

now. In a way I was right when I made a guess about the haunting, though it wouldn't have been the dear old aunt of course. Stupid of me. No wonder you never caught up with the carol-singers—I heard her, you know—I believe you did too, although you laugh at me——"

"I'm not laughing. But there were some carol-singers in costume about. A chap in the office told me. I was relieved to hear it."

"——but Lucy's a different person up there now, chatting with the others—they're terribly impressed, of course—and talking of 'different persons', do you know I think Alice was actually trying to *take over* Lucy, in more ways than one—why don't you say something?"

Her husband smiled. "For the usual reason. You rarely give anyone else a chance. But also because I'm not sure what to say. It's almost possible to explain the whole thing perfectly rationally: a lonely child, steeped in the history of the right period, her aunt had seen to that. There was even an album of old photographs to show her what it would have looked like. And then I myself told her about this house. The shock, and her strong imagination let loose. When our three were too much for her she invented a more suitable companion. All according to the book. Even when she had the urge to run away, she could blame it on someone else. The accidents fit in too——"

"But the party dress, the rocking horse——"

"Prove nothing either way. She could have unconciously have fitted them into her thoughts. But—well, I'll come clean."

"'Clean' is hardly the word for you at the moment."

172

"Exactly. I went up to the attic and opened the other trunk."

"You horrible creature! You wouldn't let us——"

"We've never had such a good reason for investigating before. It was mostly toys, obviously outgrown, and a good many old childrens' books, but I did find this——"

For the first time she saw the album open on his knee. "A scrap-book."

"*The* scrap-book. Look, Gwen." She knelt beside him. He turned the thick pages, each labelled in a small neat hand.

"Her writing was very tidy."

"Until this note at the bottom of the last filled page—*not* the last in the book, mark you."

Though the hand was clearly that of the same person, the message was scrawled in evident haste. 'Shall do no more to this book. We start a new life in the country tomorrow.' It was signed 'Alice Becket.' Under the name was an address and a date.

"Oh Pete! *Our* address. So she did live here."

"And have you noticed the date?"

She read '21st December 1873'. Their eyes met. "Today's the twenty-second," she said.

Her husband nodded. "The exact anniversary."

*　　*　　*

Upstairs the children had gone over and over the story. The more it was discussed, the more intrigued became the cousins, and the less frightening to Lucy. Alice was already becoming somebody she *used* to know. The dread of hearing her voice or her flying feet was already a thing of the past. Lucy even looked quite boldly into the mirror, confident of seeing nothing strange. It was as if Alice were quietly fading away in the same way as was that heavy threatening fog . . .

"Wake up, Lucy!" Bill bounced deliberately on the end of her bed, making her squeak because of her hand.

"Idiot," said Patrick removing Bill ungently from the bed on to the floor."

"I was only trying to brighten her up a bit!" Bill, who had landed in a heap, was aggrieved. "She's got no excuse now to——"

"And you've got no excuse to go crashing about!"

A scuffle developed. Lucy found she didn't much mind. "Boys!" was all she said to Rachel. "Useless creatures."

"All the same," said Rachel regretfully, "it was them that got you from Alice, between them."

"It was you she was most afraid of," said Lucy to comfort, but suddenly realising that this was true. "'The other one' she called you." Lucy paused. "You know, in a funny way I shall miss her."

"Don't you dare! Look what she tried to do to you. It served her right that we won."

"Won?"

"Oh yes," said Rachel calmly. "It was a sort of tug-of-war, wasn't it, between her and us?"

Was that what it had all been about?

Bill staggered from the floor, dishevelled but relatively unbattered.

"What *I* still don't see is, how it actually worked."

"All done by mirrors in the traditional manner," Patrick reminded him from where he still lay flat on his back on the floor. "Or something shiny anyway."

"But it didn't always," Bill argued. "When Lucy tried on purpose, nothing happened."

"That's why," said Rachel with a flash of inspiration. "It only worked when she wanted to be with

174

Alice. Or not with Alice. Work it out for your-selves."

Everybody thought. Everyone decided she might be right, except Lucy who was sure of it.

"You see," Patrick said triumphantly. "It all depended on what Lucy was thinking about. A matter of *reflection*, in fact."

"Oh, very funny!" said Bill scathingly.

"Not terribly," Patrick said more gravely. He jumped up. "You know we ought to be getting on with things. There's Lucy's room. And the rest of the Christmas presents to buy——"

"I haven't *any!*" wailed Lucy.

"I'll come shopping with you," said Rachel. "And you really ought to get to know some people now that you'll be coming to school with us. And if you think they wouldn't mind I'd like to come and see that Belling baby. I love them when their heads are still about to roll off."

"Ugh!" said the boys together.

"And——" Rachel suddenly remembered that she was responsible for a convalescent patient. "I say, Lucy, you look all pink. You're not getting a fever or anything are you? Perhaps we ought to go away and let you rest. After all this Christmas is going to be pretty terrific, one way and another."

"Oh please don't go. Do let's talk about it!" said Lucy.